REUBEN'S REVENGE

Reuben and Grace Chisholm led a happy, almost idyllic, life on a small homestead – until the day that was to change their lives. In the saloon, Reuben heard that their closest neighbours, the Carver family, had been murdered and their home destroyed. His first thought was for Grace, and he set off to return to her. But he was too late. The house had been burned to the ground and there was no sign of his wife. Now he must find her . . .

BEN RAY

REUBEN'S REVENGE

Complete and Unabridged

LINFORD
Leicester

First published in Great Britain in 2018 by
Robert Hale
an imprint of The Crowood Press
Wiltshire

First Linford Edition
published 2021
by arrangement with The Crowood Press
Wiltshire

*A catalogue record for this book is available
from the British Library.*

ISBN 978–1–4448–4718–5

Published by
Ulverscroft Limited
Anstey, Leicestershire

Printed and bound in Great Britain by
TJ Books Ltd., Padstow, Cornwall

This book is printed on acid-free paper

This one is for my grandson
Reuben Doyle
I can't wait for him to get old enough
to read it
Love from Grumpy Dan Dan

PROLOGUE

Reuben Chisholm loaded the buggy with supplies, helped by Silas, the store assistant. Sweat was pouring down his back as the temperature rose. Reuben took his Stetson off and, using his bandanna, wiped his head and neck.

'Sure is a hot one, Silas,' he said.

'Sure is,' Silas replied. 'All set now?'

'Yeah, thanks for your help,' Reuben said as he pulled a tarp over the supplies, securing it to the buggy. 'Think I'll grab a quick beer before I set off. Would appreciate it if you'd keep an eye on the buggy. Be seeing you next month, Silas.'

'Sure thing, Mr Chisholm.'

Reuben walked over to the nearest saloon, pushed his way through the batwings and walked up to the bar counter. 'Howdy, Reuben. Beer?' the barkeep asked.

'The colder the better, Marvin,' Reuben replied. 'Hot enough out there to fry an egg.'

Reuben downed the beer without even breathing and, wiping his mouth with the back of his hand, pushed the mug towards the barkeep. 'One more, then I must be off,' he said.

While the beer was being poured, Reuben leaned back on the bar and took a look around the saloon.

It was three in the afternoon, so the saloon was filled mostly with old-timers, nursing a beer for as long as possi.ble. Shooting the breeze and, as was their wont, sharing all the gossip.

Two men closest to Reuben were more animated than the rest, and Reuben overheard some of their conversation.

' . . . an' heard tell it was a coupla Quantrill's boys what done it,' the old-timer said.

'Yeah, I heard that too. Seems they killed the entire family and set their house aflame,' the second man said.

'Here's your beer, Reuben,' the barkeep said as he slid the glass across the bar top.

Reuben didn't seem to hear. He took

a couple of paces forward and stood by the two old-timers.

'Where'd you hear this?' he asked.

The old-timers looked up, eager to share their gossip.

'Coupla fellers riding through this morning,' one of them replied. 'I was sitting on my porch minding my own when they rode up,' he added.

'And where was this attack?' Reuben asked.

'The old Carver place, just south of here,' they seemed to answer in unison, their old, rheumy eyes appeared to sparkle as if it was the most exciting piece of gossip they'd had in years.

'I know them,' Reuben said absently, and a sudden horror flitted across his face.

The Carver spread was only three miles east of his own place, and Grace was there *on her own!*

'You tell the sheriff?' Reuben asked.

'Sure did, said he'd ride on out there later.'

'*Later!*' Reuben was disgusted. 'You

seen them two fellers before?' he asked.

'Nope. Never seen hide nor hair of 'em,' one of the men answered.

'Describe them,' Reuben said. 'Didn't you think they might be the ones responsible?'

The two men thought for a while as if getting their brains to work.

'Well,' one of them started, 'they both had big, bushy beards. Black ones, I think.'

'Nope,' the other man said. 'One of 'em was black, t'other was brown. An' he was wearing a Confederate hat, kinda dirty an' well-worn.'

'You tell the sheriff this?' Reuben asked.

'Nope, he never asked,' one of the men replied.

Reuben looked at the two men, disgust written all over his face, and then he stormed out of the saloon and ran to the sheriff's office.

He burst into the office and found the sheriff asleep in his chair, both legs resting on the desk in front of him.

4

'What the hell are you doing here?' Reuben shouted.

The sheriff sat bolt upright.

'There's been murder committed and you fall asleep?' Reuben was angrier than he'd ever been in his life.

'I ain't too well an' the doc told me to rest up some,' the sheriff replied. 'There's no way I could ride out today.'

The sheriff reached into one of the drawers in his desk and brought out some papers.

'Here's the latest batch of Wanted posters. You're welcome to them,' he said. 'You gotta excuse me, I need the John somethin' awful.'

Reuben stuffed the Wanted papers down his jeans and rushed out of the office.

He had to get home. And fast!

1

He saw the smoke when he was still a mile away from his ranch-house.

His worst fears were beginning to become a reality. He only hoped his wife had somehow managed to escape.

The closer he got, the thicker the smoke. He could see that not only was the ranch-house ablaze, but the barn as well. Any livestock in the barn would be dead before he could get anywhere near.

He reined his sweating horse and jumped from the buckboard before it had even stopped.

Running faster than he ever thought he could, he ground to a halt when he saw that his home was completely destroyed. The only remaining part of the small house was the stone chimney.

He scanned the immediate area but could see no sign of his wife.

Had she escaped, or had she been

burned to death in the house?

It was too hot for Reuben to get anywhere near the house. He stood as close as he could and peered through the curling smoke, but could not see anything resembling a body.

He noticed two sets of hoof tracks heading north and vowed to find the scum who had either taken or killed his wife, as well as destroyed his home.

Suddenly, his misery was shattered by a hail of gunshots. Self-preservation took over and he flung himself flat on the ground.

He reached for his gun but could see no target. The shots seemed to be coming from two directions. The men were still here.

But why?

All thoughts came to a halt as a slug caught the side of his head, just above his left ear.

Then everything went black.

* * *

7

Reuben had no idea how long he'd been unconscious, but the sun was slowly sinking to the west, so he figured it must have been at least an hour.

It took him a while to remember where he was, then it all flooded back to him like a huge, black, tidal wave. His head felt like a herd of buffalo had trampled it, and slowly, he sat up and took stock.

There was a pool of blood to the right of him and he remembered the shooting, then looked to his left. The full impact finally hit him, and he lowered his head as tears streaked down his face, dripping onto the arid soil.

Eventually, his crying stopped and he dry-retched for a few moments. Then he knew what he had to do. He could hardly walk. He felt as if the life had been drained out of him. But he made it to the buckboard.

He knew where his wife would have chosen to be buried if she had been killed, and he needed to do something to clear his head. He chose the flower garden she had so lovingly tended.

Taking the shovel from the buggy, he began to dig. The deeper he dug, the more his sorrow began to turn to anger.

He vowed to himself that he would find the two men who had taken his wife and burned down his house and barn — and killed Reuben on the inside.

He stuck the shovel into the loose earth when he'd finished the excavation, making sure it was deep enough to keep coyotes from digging it up and walked back to the buckboard and removed a tarp. He spread it into the empty grave.

Then he began the gruesome task he had been delaying: finding his wife's body. However, she was nowhere to be seen. No fresh mounds of earth — nothing.

He started to search again, beginning with what remained of their home, kicking at the still-smoking embers. She wasn't there. She wasn't anywhere.

Taking out the Wanted posters he scanned through them. Two men immediately caught his attention: William Clarke and Alexander Adams. The only two who vaguely resembled the old-timers' description.

From that day forth he ceased to be a small-time rancher and became a hunter.

2

That had been five years ago, and Reuben had built up a reputation of being a fair and just man and was respected by the law, and feared by the men who raped, murdered and robbed.

Wherever he was and whatever he was doing, his mind fought to answer the question: *why?* All that jumped into his mind was the day he would find his wife.

Try as he might, he couldn't get rid of the images that formed behind his closed eyes. He was forced to relive that fateful day yet again.

He'd collected bounty on a lot of fugitives, using the Wanted posters; he'd memorized every face. It wasn't just for the hell of it, it was to earn money to keep him free to hunt the two men who had his wife. He only killed when he had no choice. In the main, he liked to take his pris.oners in alive, albeit many were wounded as they stupidly tried to outgun him.

11

But in those five years, he still had not found a trace of those who had taken Grace. He'd learned from the two old-timers about their appearance, but beards could be shaved, so Reuben kept plenty of Wanted posters in his saddle-bags, the law being only too happy to keep him up to date.

Of all the posters he had, only two wore beards, and these were listed as having been with Quantrill. William Clarke and Alexander Adams!

★ ★ ★

The rain was driving almost horizontally, edged with shards of ice and slush, as the lone rider walked his horse, head bowed against the wind; bodies of both man and beast were soaked, despite the slicker and trail coat.

The man had been a-saddle for four days ever since receiving the telegram giving him the information he'd been waiting for.

He'd left Tucson, Arizona, immediately,

12

stopping only for provisions for his ride north.

The heat of Arizona had long been left behind as his journey progressed and he had not come across a single soul since leaving town.

Through slitted eyes he surveyed the territory, needing to find shelter for the night.

A flash of lightning briefly lit up a mountain range to his right, no more than two hundred yards, he reckoned; surely there would be some sort of shelter there, he thought.

Pulling on the reins, he led the animal towards the mountains, forcing his way through the strong wind and the scattering tumbleweed.

Reaching an outcrop, he headed for the lee side, pro.viding a brief respite from the wind. Lightning struck nearby, and he saw a cottonwood almost explode in flames, despite the torrential rain and slush. Again, the terrain was lit up in an eerie, blue light and he caught sight of what he hoped was a cave.

For the first time in two days, Reuben's luck was in.

The small cave was big enough for both man and horse and, after checking as best he could in the dim light that it was not already occupied by rattlers, scorpions or bears, he dismounted and led his horse inside.

He was still wary; scorpions and rattlers could hide in the smallest of places so, until he could get a fire going, was keeping his wits about him.

He took down his saddlebags and fished inside for his Lucifers, knowing in advance they would be dry, wrapped in a small tarp. Striking one, he was both pleased and amazed to see a few tumbleweed and small pieces of wood littering the cave floor.

But before building a fire, he fished out some oats and barley, tipped them into his hat, and fed the horse. The animal reached down and ate gratefully.

Keeping his stout leather gloves on, he started to shred the nearest tumbleweed, making a neat pile in the centre of the cave. Placing the small twigs and branches — mostly cottonwood, which was easy to light — he built a fire.

Within minutes, the glow of the flames lit up the cave and he was able to make out its dimensions and watch for anything crawling. What he didn't notice was that the roof of the cave was packed tight with bats. The heat and light from the fire roused them from their day-time slumber and within seconds, bats were flying everywhere.

Reuben Chisholm had faced many critters in his life: cougars, grizzlies, rattlers and scorpions, but his greatest fear had always been bats. Irrational, he knew, but somehow, they made the hair on the back of his head stand up.

He calmed himself down, taking deep breaths, picked up his Stetson and placed it under the horse's nose, encouraging him to eat.

The animal snorted, ears still pinned back tight to his head and the whites of his eyes showing as if he shared his master's fear. Gradually, the animal began to eat and he lowered the hat to the ground once more and removed his saddle.

Reuben took out his makings and rolled himself a welcome cigarette and, lighting it with a small twig from the fire — he saw no sense in wasting another Lucifer when he already had a fire — he lit up and inhaled deeply.

The tobacco took its effect and rattled nerves were calmed.

Dusk was falling and there was no let-up in the rain, but at least he had a warm, dry place to spend the night. He filled the coffee pot and set it on the fire, took out some jerky, and was content.

* * *

Come first light, Reuben sat bolt upright.

It took him a few seconds to remember where he was, and a few more before he realized the cave was full of bats, again! This time there was no wild fluttering; the bats made their way to the roof of the cave and within five minutes, silence reigned once more.

Much as he wanted a hot cup of coffee, Reuben finished the cold pot; he didn't want those bats flying around him again.

He stood and stretched his stiff limbs and looked outside. The rain had stopped and there was hardly a breath of wind. The sky was a deep blue and he could see the bright, yellow shafts of sunlight peaking over the distant eastern horizon.

Time to get going. He saddled up and led the horse outside; there would be plenty of water for his horse to drink, after three days of rain. By his reckoning, it was another two days' ride, assuming the weather held, before he reached Northfield, Minnesota. Still plenty of time.

One of Reuben's many informants had told him some.thing big was going to go down in Northfield within the next week to ten days. He didn't know what, but was certain it was a fact. Reuben had wasted no time in making tracks; he trusted his informants and they rarely let him down.

Letting his horse drink at a nearby

stream, he had time to ponder. He'd been following the Youngers up and down the West for many a month, always just missing them. Now, as Quantrill's gang had split up, it appeared they'd teamed up with the James boys. This time he was sure he'd be there before them and make sure they got the hanging they deserved.

Reuben felt the urge to clean his weapons, make sure the raging downpour hadn't damaged them. He dismounted, grabbed his saddlebags and ground-hitched his contented horse. Eight hours in the saddle and he'd made good time, but night was drawing in and he decided this was as good a place as any to set up camp. No stranger to spending the night under the stars, he only hoped the rain would keep off.

Taking out the cleaning kit he kept in his saddlebags, he almost lovingly started to clean his Colts; he removed the shells and, using an oiled rag, began to clean the chambers.

He stopped suddenly as he heard a metallic click behind him.

'I wouldn't make no sudden moves, mister, if'n I was you,' a gruff voice said, quite calmly.

'I don't intend to,' Reuben replied, equally as calm.

'Lay that pistol aside, mister, nice an' easy.'

Slowly, Reuben lowered the Colt .45 to the ground, placing it on his oily rag.

'Now, drop the gun belt,' the voice demanded.

'What in hell for?' Reuben demanded. 'There ain't no gun in it.'

'Jus' do it. OK!'

Reluctantly, Reuben unbuckled the belt and dropped it slowly to the ground. Using this as a diversion, Reuben's hand went to the boot on his right foot, feeling for the handle of his throwing knife.

He let his hand stay there, gripping the elk-horn handle.

'So, what now?' Reuben asked.

'How much money you got?'

Reuben laughed. 'Two dollars and some change,' he said.

'Shit! That all?'

'That's it, mister. Guess you struck unlucky,' Reuben said.

'We'll see 'bout that,' the stranger muttered. 'Toss that saddlebag over here.'

'Ain't nothing in there, either,' Reuben said as he threw the bag across.

As the man caught the saddlebag, the distraction was enough for Reuben to throw the knife.

His aim was true. Not wanting to kill the man, Reuben had figured to hit the right shoulder — the man's gun arm — and he succeeded as, with a yelp, the man involuntarily lost control of his gun, loosing off a shot that bit harmlessly into the ground.

Reuben leapt to his feet and rushed the man, pinning him to the ground, before extracting the knife. He wiped the blood from it onto the man's shirt and pressed the blade to the man's neck.

'If you're gonna kill me, get it over with,' the stranger said through gritted teeth.

'If I was gonna kill you, you'd be dead by now,' Reuben said. 'And what were you planning to do?'

'Well, I weren't plannin' on killin' any-one. I got bushwhacked five days ago. Lost everythin', food, water, ammo an' my horse. All they left me with was that handgun with one slug in it. Been walkin' most of the time an' not found a thing to eat. I'm sorry, mister, guess I was just gettin' to the end of my tether.'

Reuben re-sheathed the knife and stood up. 'Better take a look at that shoulder.'

The man struggled to his feet and started to take off his trail coat. That was as far as he got.

From out of nowhere, a shot rang out, hitting him square in the back. The force of the slug sent him flying forwards to land face-down in the camp-fire.

Reuben grabbed the man's legs and started to pull him free of the flames, but knew it was already too late. The stench of burning flesh filled his nostrils, the man's long, dank hair was well alight, and he almost threw up.

Reuben was exposed; silhouetted by

the camp-fire, he was an easy target for the hidden bushwhacker. He dived to his left as another shot rang out, sending a plume of dust and sand over Reuben's face.

He could see his rifle lying next to his saddle, and his Peacemaker was where he'd placed it while cleaning it, but how the hell could he get to them?

Working his way snakelike across the ground, Reuben kept the camp-fire between himself and the unseen attacker. Keeping low and flat, Reuben made a grab for the Winchester and pulled it quickly towards him. Then he waited.

He didn't have to wait long.

A third shot was fired, and the camp-fire erupted as the slug hit it, sending sparks high into the night sky. But he had seen the muzzle flash, and now had something to aim at. Sighting down the long barrel of the Winchester .44.40, with its extra rear sight for greater accuracy, he gently squeezed the trigger.

His shot was instantly rewarded. A yelp of pain followed by a long, low grunt, told its own story. He had at least hit the bushwhacker

Reuben waited for a full five minutes; he wasn't about to assume that he had killed his attacker, so held back, not making any move. He was just about to relax some when another shot thudded into the dirt beside him.

'Shit! There's more than one!' Reuben had missed where the shot had come from so stayed where he was, his eyes darting every which way to get some clue as to where the second shooter was.

It was eerily quiet. Reuben could hear the beating of his own heart as he awaited the next shot. Again, he didn't have to wait long.

This time, he felt the slug sear across his back without biting into flesh. But he felt his coat pull as the bullet passed through it.

On this occasion, he did see the flash of the other shooter and that was enough.

Reuben rolled several times to his left before raising the Winchester once more. There was no time to take a careful aim, so he fired in the general direction of the last muzzle flash, and ducked down low again.

There was no return fire.

Reuben kept his head down in case the bushwhacker was playing possum. Slowly, he inched his way backwards, away from the fire and into relative darkness.

The wind began to pick up and Reuben hoped it wasn't a sign of the rain returning. His slicker was behind his saddle, wrapped around his bedroll, but the horse was a good thirty feet away on the other side of the camp-fire.

For twenty minutes Reuben didn't move a muscle, then he heard, rather than saw, a horse galloping off. He hoped it wasn't his.

A shot, miles wide of him, was fired and Reuben knew his attacker had decided to vamoose. The fool was silhouetted against a dull, yellow moon and Reuben took careful aim with the .44.40.

The rider slumped forward in his saddle then slid to one side, and as he hit the dirt, a foot caught in a stirrup as the horse bolted.

The animal lurched to its left and Reuben was able to see the fallen body being pummelled against rocks. The only sound was the clank of metal shoes on the hard ground.

The dragged rider didn't utter a sound.

Reuben stood now, watching the horse and late rider fade into the distance, before turning his attention to the first shooter.

Crouching down to present a smaller target should the man still be alive, Reuben edged forwards. He had no choice but to circumnavigate the camp-fire, putting himself in possible danger, but he needn't have worried.

On reaching the first shooter he could see quite plainly that the man was dead. He'd taken a .44.40 slug to the side of the head. The bullet had shattered his skull before exiting and burying itself in the ground.

Bending over the corpse, Reuben took a long look at what was left of the man's face. He didn't recognize him at all. Turning the body over, Reuben went through the man's pockets, looking for a clue as to who he was, but found nothing except a baccy bag and papers.

Two chancers, Reuben thought. Certainly no one he'd tracked before, seeking revenge.

*   *   *

A horse neighed in front of Reuben, no more than ten feet away. The animal seemed unconcerned with the gunplay as it chomped on a patch of coarse grass.

He patted the animal's neck, talking softly as he did so. He lifted off the saddlebags to see if there was anything of use inside. To his delight he found food and a bottle of bourbon. OK, so the food was only jerky, some fat-back bacon and beans, but also a full tin of Arbuckle's. Reuben couldn't help but smile.

He took the saddlebag to the campfire, then returned to the horse, which was ground-hitched, and released the reins; the animal stayed where it was, so he left it to forage.

Next, he took the dead man's rifle, his Colt and all his ammo. 'More use to me than you, buster,' Reuben said. He had little sympathy for the dead man. Bush-whackers and back-shooters were, in his book, the lowest of the low.

He took another long, good look at the dead man, but could swear he'd never seen him before. Perhaps he was kin to someone Reuben had apprehended. He'd never know.

'Critters'll take care of you and, come sunlight, the buzzards will take what's left. Good riddance!'

Grabbing his bedroll and slicker, Reuben set up the rest of the camp, built the fire, then fed his horse some oats and barley before leading him to a patch of grass where he ground-hitched him. He removed his saddle and rubbed the animal down. 'There you go, boy, all set for a night's sleep.' He patted the animal's rump and returned to the camp-fire.

He filled the coffee pot with water from

the stream and, when it boiled, added a generous amount of Arbuckle's and set that to brew as he filled a pan with beans and some of the bacon, then leaned back on his saddle and rolled a quirley.

This was turning out to be a fine night after all, Reuben thought to himself. He finished his cigarette and poured a cup of coffee, then using the last of his bread, mopped up the beans and bacon, scraping every last ounce of bacon fat from the pan.

* * *

The night passed peacefully, and Reuben was grateful that the rain had held off.

He had already decided to bury, as best he could, the man who had tried to rob him initially and been unlucky enough to get himself killed by the bushwhackers.

The best he could do was cover the body with rocks and stones. He knew coyotes and buzzards would take little time in getting at the body, but without any digging implements, it was his only option.

When he'd finished, he brewed up some more coffee and set to work getting ready to resume his journey. Once packed, coffee drained, he mounted up and set off for Northfield, Minnesota.

3

Frank and Jesse James led their gang out of Missouri and into Minnesota. They had been planning to rob the First National Bank in Mankato, but Jesse was spotted as he rode down the main street, so he and the gang, which con.sisted of the three Younger brothers, Cole, Jim and Bob, and four ex-Quantrill raiders, Clell Miller, Charlie Pitts, Bill Chadwell and 'Bloody' Bill Anderson, rode north and headed for Northfield.

Frank and Jesse had been thorough in their search for the right bank to rob, having visited ten cities — mostly by rail — and posed as a party of land speculators, which gave them ample opportunity to familiarize themselves with the various banks they inspected, as well as plan possible escape routes.

It was Chadwell's idea to go to Northfield. He knew the town was prosperous, and they had a large bank there on

Division Street.

'Reckon I'll ride on ahead,' Chadwell said. 'Do a recce on the place.'

'Good idea,' Jesse agreed. 'Find out everything you can about the place. Cole, you go with him.'

'OK, Jesse,' Cole Younger replied.

'We'll meet at that inn we just passed, come sundown.'

Chadwell agreed and the two men set off for Northfield.

On reaching the town, Chadwell and Younger dismounted on Division Street. Chadwell lit a small cigar and looked up and down the thoroughfare.

'Wait here with the horses,' he said to Cole. 'I'll take a look round, see what I can find out.'

Cole rolled a cigarette and nodded.

'Hey, mister,' Chadwell called out to a passer-by. 'Any gun shops in town?'

'Hell no, we don't have a single one,' the man replied without breaking stride.

Chadwell then headed to the first of two hardware stores, but they held little of interest to him.

He stepped out onto the boardwalk, stomped his cigar out and took a leisurely stroll towards the bank. He crossed the iron bridge that spanned the Cannon River, and turned right onto Mill Square.

The two-storey Scriver Block housed some stores, as well as the First National Bank. The bank's main entrance was not on the Square, but around the corner on Division Street. Chadwell, not wishing to draw attention to himself, didn't stop to scrutinise the building, but nevertheless took in the whole scene.

He headed back to Cole.

'Seems easy enough,' Chadwell told Cole, 'no permanent law here either; they must be pretty damn sure of themselves in these parts.'

'We heading to the inn now?' Cole asked, not making any comment about the bank or the town.

'Yeah, not much point in sticking around here. Before we go, I'll do a rough plan of the area for Frank and Jesse.

Chadwell pulled a small piece of paper from his vest pocket, along with a stub of pencil and drew a plan of the square, showing the bank's front and rear doors and the two streets leading into the square.

Satisfied with his map, he put it back in his vest pocket. 'There's two ways into town, and that means there's two ways out, too,' Chadwell said as he hefted his bulky frame aboard his horse and pulled rein.

★ ★ ★

Although the wind was still gusty, there had so far only been a light drizzle as Reuben headed north. He kept his eyes and ears alert, checking his back-trail in case any bushwhackers were following.

With the ground damp there would be no tell-tale dust kicked up by anyone behind him, so he had to rely on his hearing. Metal on stone would carry in this wind.

Satisfied — for the time being — that no one was tracking him, Reuben decided it was time to stop and eat.

He reached an outcrop that provided some shelter from the wind and was reasonably dry. Dismounting, he took down his canteen and poured half the contents into his Stetson and let his horse drink. Then, reaching into his war bag that hung from his pommel, he grabbed a handful of barley and scattered it on some coarse-looking grass that would satisfy his horse for a while.

Collecting some tumbleweed, he crunched it up, boost.ing it with small twigs trapped near the boulder he was standing by, and lit a fire, adding more twigs as the flames took hold. Planting a larger twig over the fire, he filled the coffee pot and waited for the water to boil.

Then he remembered the bourbon! 'That would warm a body up some,' he said aloud, causing the horse to stop eating and look up at him.

'It's OK, boy,' he said, 'only a couple of swigs.' The horse bent low and continued eating as if he understood what his master had said. Reuben almost believed he had.

With the water close to boiling, Reuben dug out his pan and put the rest of the fat-back bacon in it and placed it on the fire. Within minutes, the smell of cooking bacon was making his mouth water. He added some beans, and rolled a cigarette while he waited for the food to cook. Some Arbuckle's in the pot, and he was set.

The wind had dropped slightly, and the drizzle had mostly halted. Reuben lit his cigarette, once more a con.tented man.

Five minutes later, he was scooping out beans and bacon with the last of his bread, washing it down with fresh coffee. All the time he was thinking, *it doesn't get much better than this!*

There was enough coffee left for one more mouthful, to which he added a splash of bourbon and downed it in one swallow.

He was sorely tempted to pull his Stetson down over his face and take a nap but considered that to be dangerous. He'd been shot at twice and didn't want a third time.

Standing, he tossed the coffee grains on the fire, kicked sand over it to make sure it was out, rinsed both the coffee pot and mug with sand, and did the same with the pan before stowing them in his saddlebag.

'Time to move on, boy,' he said, mounting up. The horse snickered in reply.

The drizzle had petered out and the wind was dropping by the second. Here and there were bright patches of blue sky surrounded by cotton-wool clouds. It was cold, but the day was now bright as the sun appeared, throwing down the little heat it held at this time of year.

The terrain that stretched before him was flat, the ground drying rapidly, and he set the horse to an easy lope, letting the animal pick its own route between patches of coarse grass, cactus, Joshua trees and cotton.woods.

Reuben constantly scanned ahead and behind him; always paid to be careful. Although he saw and heard nothing out of the ordinary, Reuben was certain he was being watched. Where and by whom, he didn't know, but his gut feeling rarely let him down.

It didn't this time either.

Out of the corner of his eye, Reuben caught sight of a flash of light. It only lasted for a second or two, but was enough to warn him. The flash came again; someone was getting ready to shoot at him.

Reuben dug his heels in and the startled horse immediately leapt into a gallop. Reuben wanted to put as much distance between himself and the bushwhacker as possible.

He heard the distant crack as the gun was fired, but the shooter was well out of range. Reuben saw a small plume of sand rise as the slug hit the ground harmlessly. He reined in and turned his horse to face the gunman. Scanning the terrain to locate the man; he needed to get a fix on his position. *This is going to end here,* Reuben thought to himself, *I ain't gonna be dogged all the way to Northfield.*

Sliding his .44.40 from the scabbard, Reuben dismounted and waited for the man's next move. He caught sight of another brief flash of light. The man's an idiot, Reuben thought. *He sure ain't no gunman, that's for sure.*

Cocking the Winchester, Reuben raised it to his right shoulder, setting the butt comfortably, and sighted down the barrel. He wasn't sure if the weapon would reach its target, but it would be pretty close.

Holding his breath, Reuben started to squeeze the trigger. The bullet exploded from the rifle, and Reuben's shoulder coped easily with the expected recoil.

Lowering the gun, he stared into the distance. There was no return fire, but that didn't mean he'd found his target.

'Stay here, boy,' he said to his horse as he ground-hitched it. The animal seemed unconcerned and fell to his favourite pastime of grazing.

Holding the rifle hip high, Reuben started to walk towards the hidden bushwhacker, ready to shoot if the need arose. He figured the distance was still over two hundred yards to where he'd seen the reflected flashes, still too far to be certain of a hit, let alone a fatal one.

Slowly but surely, Reuben walked forwards expecting a shot to head his way at any moment. The silence was ominous, almost deafening. *Who the hell was trying to kill him, and why?*

No shots came.

He was around one hundred fifty yards away now and Reuben knew for sure that if he saw his quarry he could hit it.

Crouching slightly to present a smaller target of himself, he thought he heard movement. Reuben stopped. Ears straining to catch the slightest noise.

Ahead, a patch of tall grass with cactus fighting for space would be a good hiding place for the bushwhacker.

And so it proved.

From behind a giant Saguaro, a figure appeared, rifle aimed.

Reuben didn't hesitate. Firing from the hip, he loosed two quick shots. Both found their target as the man was thrown backwards into the tall grass.

Cocking the Winchester once more, Reuben kicked his way through the grass and stood staring at the body of yet another man he had never seen before. The man wasn't dead — yet.

Reuben could see that one slug had gut shot him, the other high up near the right shoulder. The bushwhacker's eyes were glazed. Blood seeped from one corner of his mouth and his trail coat was soaked.

'Why'd you try to kill me, man?' Reuben asked, bending low.

The man spit blood, but didn't answer. His left hand was searching the ground in a futile attempt to find his rifle.

'Ain't no use you groping around, fella. You're as good as dead,' Reuben said without emotion.

The man coughed, wincing in pain as more blood spewed from his mouth. His breath was coming in short pants until they slowed and finally stopped.

'Damn you to hell, fella!' Reuben

almost shouted. For the third time in a little over twenty-four hours, Reuben was searching a dead man's pockets for any clue as to his identity. Once again, there was nothing. It certainly wasn't Clarke or Adams, of that he was certain.

'Guess I'll never know the who or the why now,' Reuben said, then whistled for his horse.

The animal stopped grazing and raised its head, looking in Reuben's direction. It seemed to sigh, not liking the interruption, and began to walk lazily towards Reuben. There was no way it was going to rush.

As soon as he saw it move, Reuben knew the animal was sulking, so he whistled again.

The horse totally ignored him and continued to walk, taking its own sweet time.

'Ornery cuss,' Reuben mouthed and started to head towards the horse, in boots that were not made for walking.

4

Frank and Jesse James were playing poker with Jim and Bob Younger, Clell Miller and Charlie Pitts at an inn three miles outside Northfield. The inn was a popular haunt as it was at the junction of two trails; one north-south, the other east-west, so a lot of trading was done there.

The James gang had already gone through one bottle of imported whisky — not for them the cheap rotgut that could take the varnish off furniture! But Frank and Jesse would not let the gang get drunk and maybe shoot their mouths off or, worse, their guns.

The idea was not to draw attention to themselves, and although Charlie Pitts complained bitterly, one look from Jesse and he shut up. He'd seen that look before.

'How long you reckon afore Cole and Bill get here?' Clell asked, lighting a cigar.

'Reckon it'll be sunset at the earliest,' Frank surmised. 'As long as they don't cause no suspicion.'

'Well, let's hope Bill was right about the First National, I'll sure be a tad ruffled if it all comes to nought!' Jesse said, sipping the last of his whisky. 'We need the cash, then maybe, we can head south for the winter, get out of this cold. Maybe as far as Californy, I hear it's pretty warm in those parts.'

'We've known Bill for a while now, I respect his judge.ment,' Frank said.

'Me, too,' Jesse added. 'If Bill is satisfied with the set-up, we'll move in. If not, well, I'll worry about that when and if it happens.'

Frank stood and walked to the bar, Charlie Pitts licked his lips, thinking another bottle was coming.

'Coffee, lots of it,' Frank ordered and returned to his seat.

Charlie Pitts was a disappointed man.

* * *

Reuben grabbed the reins of his horse and hauled himself aboard.

'Thanks for nothing,' he said to his horse. 'As if I ain't had enough trouble today without you sulking out on me.'

The horse merely snorted. If Reuben didn't know better, he would have thought it was a snort of contempt! In fact, the more he thought about it the more he was convinced that was exactly what it was.

'You're too damn smart for your own good, boy,' he said, and rubbed the animal's neck. Pulling on the reins, he wheeled the horse around and set off for Northfield. 'Let's see if we can have an uninterrupted journey for a change.'

Digging his heels into the horse's flanks he said, 'About time you had a good gallop, boy. Get some of that feistiness outa your system.'

The warmth of the late afternoon sun made a pleasant change from the previous few days of strong winds and rain. There was still a chill in the air and, pretty soon, Reuben knew the snow would start, heralding winter's arrival. Travel would be all but impossible except for the seasoned trappers, the hard men of the West. It would take an earthquake or hurricane to stop them.

After thirty minutes of hard riding, Reuben slowed his horse down to a canter. He reckoned he'd covered a good ten to fifteen uneventful miles — at least no one had taken a shot at him. Reuben smiled, relieved, but he didn't let his guard down. He still checked his back trail and scanned the territory, looking for any sign that might spell trouble.

It was late afternoon, and to the west the sun was sinking ever lower and the temperature began to fall dramatically. The breeze started to gust into a wind and tumbleweed began to roll, forever searching for a place to rest and germinate again.

In a matter of minutes, the sun disappeared behind the distant horizon and darkness fell. Although there was a full moon, the black clouds scudding across the sky almost obliterated any light it might have shed.

Reuben let the horse have its head, trusting it to be sure-footed. The last thing he needed was a lame horse.

Reuben realized he wouldn't reach Northfield tonight, so instead steered to Rochester, about fifty miles south of Northfield; if he left at first light, he'd reach Northfield by mid-morning easily.

Tired, hungry and cold, even his horse seemed to brighten up, snorting and flicking his head, he appeared to prance across the plain.

'You can smell it, can't you, boy,' Reuben said, patting the animal's neck.

The horse snorted again, nodding his head up and down in answer.

Without being prompted, the horse picked up its pace. Not quite a full-on gallop, but not far off.

'Easy, boy. Better to get there safely, then you can have all the barley and water you want.'

Chisholm reached the outskirts of Rochester at six o'clock in the evening. The town's street lights didn't start for another two hundred or so yards, so he assumed this part of town was the lower end.

The assorted shacks were unkempt, with no yards, back or front, rubbish scattered everywhere. It looked that no one cared about anything.

Reaching the start of the street lights, the atmosphere changed dramatically.

There was no trash littering the main drag, it even looked as if the street had been raked smooth. The houses were neat and tidy with small, white, pick-et-fenced yards to the front and rear. The boardwalks outside the various businesses were spotless. The contrast was amazing.

Up ahead, Reuben could hear the tinkling of a piano from one of the saloons and the soft, melodious voice of what, Reuben thought, must be an angel singing.

He couldn't help but smile and felt a surge of peacefulness pass through him for the first time since . . . .

He tried hard not to think back to the

time he'd lost his wife, and imagined her raped and murdered. Reuben shook his head as if to dispel the thoughts that were build.ing up in his head.

But he couldn't stop them.

He rode on till he found the livery. The old-timer in charge looked up from the newspaper he was reading as Reuben dismounted.

'Howdy, stranger,' the old man said.

'Howdy to you, too,' Reuben replied. 'Needs a rub down and some food and water for the night. You got room?'

The old-timer took in Reuben's appearance, noting the low-slung side iron on his right thigh set for a cross draw, the steely, blue eyes set either side of an aquiline nose over a firm, square jaw and the muscular frame of a man who could sure take care of himself — with fists or gunplay.

'Just the one night?' the ostler asked.

'Yep, heading out at first light,' Reuben replied.

'Heading north?'

'You seem mighty interested in my arrangements, old-timer,' Reuben said.

48

'Nah, just conversation, I'm naturally nosey.'

'What's your name?' Reuben asked.

'Sam. And yours?'

'Reuben.'

'Well, Reuben, I'll take real good care of your hoss, he'll be as snug as a bug in a rug. It'll be two dollars for the stall, grooming and feed.'

Reuben gave the old man three dollars. 'You take extra care of him, OK?'

'Sure as eggs is eggs, Reuben.'

'Recommend a rooming-house?' Reuben asked.

'Sure. Three blocks down, first on the left. Mrs Brown'll take care of ya, and her cooking's the finest you'll ever taste.'

''Preciate it, see you at first light.' Reuben tipped his Stetson and grabbed his saddlebags and headed off.

Being a bounty hunter, Reuben didn't spend much time in towns. All he ever did was bring fugitives in, leave his bank details, and leave. He found that he had an aversion to too many people being around.

The night air was cool, a fresh breeze was blowing off the prairie to the south and it felt bracing after the mug.giness of the day. What he needed now was a shave, haircut and bath, followed by a bellyful of food and then, maybe a few beers.

The red, white and blue barber's pole beckoned, and Reuben entered.

'Howdy, mister,' the barber put down the paper he was reading. 'What'll it be? But by the look of you, you need the full treatment,' he said and laughed.

'Sure do, and a hot tub,' Reuben replied, taking off his Stetson and placing his saddlebags on the floor by the barber chair.

His hair cut and face shaved, he looked and felt like a new man.

'Now to get outta these trail-dust clothes,' Reuben said as the barber showed him the back of his head in a small, hand-held mirror.

'How's that?' he asked.

Reuben studied the reflection and nodded: 'Sure looks fine to me,' he said.

'Tub'll be ten minutes, there's a newspaper there while you wait.' The barber went into a back room.

Reuben picked up the paper, the *Post-Bulletin*, and flicked through the four pages. His attention was caught by a small article on the front page.

Unconfirmed reports are coming in. Eyewitnesses say they saw the James-Younger gang heading north, probably heading towards Northfield.

As mentioned, these reports are not confirmed but the *Post-Bulletin* will keep you informed.

And that was it. A short six lines, concerning the most notorious gang in America. Even the millinery store had more words describing its winter sale! Reuben flicked through the pages again in case he'd missed something, but there was no further news of any interest.

'Tub's ready,' the barber called out, and Reuben grabbed his saddlebags, eager to get washed and changed, his stomach rumbling in protest with the need for some grub and a cool beer or two.

Reuben luxuriated in the tub for a tad longer than he needed, but felt his muscles relax in the warm water and he sure smelled a lot better!

Drying himself off, he changed into clean clothes — throwing his trail-dusty clothes away; he'd buy more later. Feeling like a new man, he paid the barber, grabbed his saddlebags and headed to Mrs Brown's boarding-house.

She was a small, plump woman, mid-fifties, Reuben guessed, but she had a twinkle in her large, brown eyes and he could tell she'd been a beauty when she was younger.

'Howdy, ma'am, was told by Sam you might have a room available,' Reuben said.

She eyed him from top to toe before answering the tall, dark-haired stranger. He seemed to pass muster, as she smiled sweetly, showing white, even teeth and the sparkle in her eyes seemed to grow brighter.

'Sure have, mister,' she replied, opening the door wider to let him in.

As he passed, she straightened her dress and patted her hair and said: 'I'm Mrs Brown, but you can call me Molly.'

'Pleasure to meet you, Molly. I'm Reuben Chisholm, please call me Reuben.'

'Are you staying long?' she enquired.

'One night, maybe two at the most,' Reuben replied.

The look of disappointment on Molly's face was far too obvious. She pulled her smile back and became more businesslike.

'Room's two dollars a night, includes supper, and I got fresh beef, taters, greens, gravy and biscuits, if'n you're a mind to it.'

'Ma'am — Molly, that sounds like a fine feast, I ain't eaten in a while,' Reuben said and removed his Stetson.

'I'll show you your room, supper'll be ready in thirty minutes.'

'I'll be right ready,' Reuben said with a grin.

Reuben entered the small but

53

comfortable-looking room.

To his left was a large window that looked out over Main Street. Immediately in front of him was the bed with an eiderdown and two large pillows.

'Sure beats sleeping rough,' Reuben said aloud as he hung his saddlebags on the bed post and surveyed the rest of the room.

A chest of drawers stood against the far wall and a pitcher, bowl, towel — even a bar of soap — was arranged neatly on top.

Reuben's sense of well-being was rudely shaken as the large glass window exploded, sending shards of jagged glass all over the room. Instinctively, Reuben dropped to the floor, his Colt already drawn.

He heard the dull thud as the slug punched a hole in the far wall.

Molly burst into the room: 'What on earth . . . ' but she stopped speaking as she saw the shattered window and Reuben lying prone on the floor.

'Get back,' Reuben shouted, 'there's a

shooter out there.'

Molly ducked back out of the room but stood in the doorway.

Another shot thudded into the far wall, narrowly missing the pitcher and bowl.

'I'm going for the sheriff,' Molly said.

'Wait, is there another room that faces Main?' Reuben asked.

'Across the hall here,' Molly replied.

'I'm gonna see if I can get a bead on the shooter,' Reuben said, and began to edge backwards towards the door.

'Leave by the back door,' Reuben said, 'don't want you shot by mistake.'

Reuben watched Molly until she reached the end of the hallway and descended the stairs. He then quietly opened the door to the room opposite his and took a step inside.

Another large window stood to his right, the room was a mirror image of his own. Keeping low, he walked to the side of the window and took a quick look at Main Street.

It was, as he expected, deserted. He

could see move.ment in one of the stores opposite the boarding-house, but Reuben knew, from the angle the bullets had entered his room, that the shooter was on a rooftop somewhere. He wasn't shooting up into the room but level with it.

The question was, where was he now? It was answered as another shot was fired into Reuben's room.

Reuben caught sight of a hat and a rifle for the briefest of moments, but at least it gave him something to aim at. Slowly, he raised the window, just six inches, and rested the barrel of the Colt on the windowsill.

Reuben aimed for the façade just below where he'd seen the hat, knowing that the slug would easily penetrate the thin clapboard. His right index finger caressed the trigger slowly, feeling the tension in the mechanism until the hammer fell and the slug erupted from the muzzle.

The explosion from the gun was highlighted by the silence of the street and,

56

as the black powder smoke cleared, Reuben heard a yelp of pain from across the street.

As Reuben stood, he felt a sharp prod in his back. 'Hold it right there, mister,' a voice ordered. 'Lose that weapon and raise 'em high,' the voice went on.

'You got it all wrong, Sheriff — ' Reuben began.

'I ain't no sheriff,' the voice came, gruff and thick. Reuben could feel the hatred emanating from the man behind him.

'Then who the hell are you?' Reuben demanded.

'All in good time,' the man replied.

That was the last thing Reuben heard. The last thing he felt was a sharp blow to the back of his head. Then blackness engulfed him.

5

Opening one eye, all Reuben could see was darkness. His head thundered, and he winced at the pain. He soon discovered his hands and feet were bound tightly and it was almost impossible to move.

Who the hell were these people? He knew there must be more than one as they'd carted his body from the rooming-house to wherever he was now.

And what happened to the sheriff?

Dragging himself back to consciousness, Reuben turned onto his side. It took him a few minutes to remember what had happened. He tried to stand, but his hands and feet were becoming numb as the tight ropes slowed the blood flow.

Bending his legs back towards his bound hands, he tried to reach his right boot, hoping against hope that the small throwing knife he always carried was still there.

His fingertips reached the top of his boot, and strain.ing, the rope cutting into his wrists, he stretched an inch further and felt the shaft of the handle.

Gripping with just two fingers, he slowly began to pull.

He'd raised it by about an inch and was finally able to use his thumb and forefinger to pull the knife clear of his boot.

Reuben relaxed, a firm grip on the knife. The effort had made him sweat and he felt it running down his face.

Now for the hard part.

Gripping the elk horn handle tightly, Reuben began to saw at the ropes binding him.

The sweat was pouring off him by now; he felt it running down his chest, back, face and arms, although he wasn't sure whether the sweat on his hands was blood as his numb hand continued sawing.

He felt the rope loosen slightly, but didn't know if it was wishful thinking. It wasn't. He pulled his wrists apart as hard as he could. The pain was excruciating, but the rope suddenly went slack.

His hands were free and he felt the blood rushing through his veins as pins and needles took over. He'd have to wait a while before he could undo the rope holding his legs together.

Breathing deeply and slowly, he calmed his body as the pins and needles faded and feeling came back into his hands.

His wrists were a bloody mess from both the rope and where he'd caught his flesh with the knife. He untied his bandanna and ripped it in half, wrapping each half round his wrists. It would have to do until he could see a doc.

He leant forward and untied the ropes binding his legs, then reached for his holster.

It was empty.

He replaced the knife in his boot and stood on weak legs, again, pins and needles as the blood rushed through.

He surveyed his surroundings. It was pitch black and he could make little out. So he began to feel round the walls. There had to be a door.

His hip felt something: a handle. He knew it would be locked, but he turned it anyway. To his surprise, the door opened; light flooded in, blinding him temporarily.

He looked back inside the room and saw a table and two chairs. His gun was on the table.

Now armed, he stepped outside.

He scanned the horizon and saw the town, at least three or four miles away. Reuben then walked round the small shack.

He couldn't believe his eyes. His horse was ground tethered!

These boys are pure amateurs, he thought to himself. Either that or they thought he stood no chance of escaping.

Cautiously he surveyed the terrain. The land was flat, no trees or rocky hills to hide behind.

Reuben was puzzled. He had no idea who had bush-whacked him — or why. He still had his horse, his weapons and, lifting the flap of his saddlebags, could see that nothing had been taken from it.

He mounted up, hoping there would be some tracks to follow, but the ground was hard. There were one or two hoof prints, but little else to follow. Seemed like he'd never know who'd hit him.

Deciding not to go back to his room at Molly's place, he headed north.

Northfield couldn't be that far away now.

Perhaps the answers were there.

6

By pure coincidence, just as Cole Younger and Bill Chadwell left Northfield, Reuben Chisholm arrived.

Reuben's first port of call was to find a hotel, and that didn't take long. Crossing the iron bridge he saw a sign for a hotel called the Dampier House, situated in the Scriver Block. He walked his horse to the hotel and tied him to the hitch rail. He removed his saddlebag and entered the hotel.

There was no one in the foyer, or at the reception desk, but a small bell and two wooden signs. One said: Henry Potter manager. The other said: Please ring for attention.

So he did.

Within a minute a portly, middle-aged man appeared, smiling and sliding a pair of spectacles onto his nose.

'Sir, how may I help you?' he asked.

'You got a room?'

63

'Certainly, sir. They start at five dollars a night, or we have one fifteen-dollar room available.'

'The five-dollar room will suffice,' Reuben said. 'Is there a livery nearby?'

'We can handle that for you, sir, one dollar for the stall, seventy-five cents for feed and grooming, although most folks tip the young ostler if they think he's done a good job.'

'Fair enough,' Reuben agreed.

'The room you pay in advance, the livery when you leave. How long you planning on staying?'

'Ain't too sure. Maybe two or three nights, but I'll pay for tonight first. That OK?'

'That will be fine, Mr Er — ?'

'Chisholm. Reuben Chisholm.'

'Mr Chisholm, if you'd like to sign the register . . . "

Reuben signed then asked, 'Where's a good place to eat, hereabouts?'

'Well, there's J.G. Jefts, just across the bridge yonder. They do a pretty good steak,' the receptionist said.

Handing over the five dollars, Reuben took the key to his room from Potter.

'Number seven, it's on the first floor, last door on the right. Enjoy your stay, Mr Chisholm.'

Reuben tipped his hat, slung his saddlebag over his shoulder and headed for the stairs at the far end of the foyer.

Reaching room number seven, he found the door unlocked. No surprise, he guessed, the room was empty. Entering, he took a look round to see what his five dollars had paid for.

On the far wall facing the door was a three-quarter size bed. Two white pillows and a thick eiderdown cover. *Now that, I'm looking forward to*, he thought. To the right of the bed was a three-drawer dresser with a wash bowl, water jug, a hand towel and a small tablet of soap. To the left of the bed, a small rug and a window, the drapes closed. Reuben opened them to reveal a back alley in near darkness. He closed them again.

Placing his saddlebag on the bed, he took off his Stetson then poured some water into the bowl. He took off his shirt and washed his hands and face thoroughly; drying himself off, he reached into his saddlebag and took out a fresh shirt.

Feeling more human now, the hunger in his belly surfaced so he made his way over to the eating-house, eager to taste that steak.

* * *

Cole Younger and Bill Chadwell rode at a leisurely pace to the inn to meet up with the rest of the gang. Chadwell, in particular, was all for robbing the First National bank in Northfield. It would be like taking candy from a baby.

He smiled at that thought, then reached into his vest pocket and pulled out a cheroot. Reining in, he struck a Lucifer with his thumb and inhaled the acrid smoke deeply. Then coughed just as deeply.

After this raid, he thought, nothing but the finest Cuban cigars, not these horse-shit cheroots. But he continued to smoke it anyway. In his mind he could see a bevy of beautiful women at his beck and call. Fine French brandy, real Scotch whisky. What more could a man desire?

'You gonna sit there all night with that stupid grin on your face?' Cole said.

'Just daydreaming, boy. Just daydreaming. Come on, let's ride.' Chadwell gripped the cheroot with his teeth and dug his spurs in.

Cole didn't follow straight away. He sighed, shook his head from side to side then just said, 'Giddup,' to his horse. He was beginning to distrust Chadwell and his judgement.

It was thirty minutes later that they reached the inn. It all seemed quiet — too quiet. No raucous laughter: no honky-tonk piano, nothing.

Cole and Chadwell dismounted and tethered their animals. Cole already had his Peacemaker in his hand. Both men were cautious as they approached the batwings of the inn.

Cole went to the right and Chadwell to the left and slowly both men leant forwards to take a looksee, their guns cocked and ready to fire.

What they saw made both men feel a little embarrassed.

The inn was practically deserted, the James-Younger gang being the only patrons, and they were drinking coffee.

Cole and Chadwell holstered their weapons and walked in.

The metallic click when the two men released the hammer on their guns was enough for both Frank and Jesse to draw their pistols ready to shoot.

Another second and they would have, but in the dim light they saw who had entered.

'About time you two got here,' Frank said.

'How's it lookin'?' Jesse asked. 'Do we take it or move on out?'

'It's looking good, Jesse. The bank's main entrance is in Division Street, and there's a back entrance that leads to the square. In the same building, it's called the Scriver Block, there's a couple of small businesses, nothing to worry about. Here, I drew this map.' And he handed it to Jesse.

Jesse was keen on this raid, but the rest of the gang had their reservations.

'Opposite the main entrance to the bank there's a small hotel, a drugstore and a row of small commercial buildings again, nothing to worry about there.' Chadwell waited to hear what Frank and Jesse had to say and beckoned the bartender. 'Whiskey,' he said.

'Just the one, Bill, we all need to keep a clear head,' Frank said.

'I'll take one too then,' Cole said, and pulled a chair up to the table.

'OK, here's what I figure. Tomorrow at around noon, me, Charlie and Bob will ride into Northfield and do a recce, see how many folks there are around, get the lie of the land and make sure there are no potential hazards that weren't there today.

'Now, if all looks to be OK, we'll hitch our horses outside the main entrance to the bank. That's when we create a diversion.'

'How're we gonna do that, fer Chris'sakes?' It was Clell Miller who spoke out, instantly regretting it.

Jesse gave him a cold, hard look but didn't answer straight away.

'I want you, Frank, Bill and Cole, to come into Northfield at exactly two o'clock, across the iron bridge, a-whoopin' and a-hollerin'. Then Jim and Clell, you do the same but down Division Street so we's got cover and backup, while me, Charlie and Bob rob the bank.'

He paused.

'Me, Charlie and Bob will head for the bank; there should be enough chaos outside to hide what we're doin' inside the bank.' Jesse looked at each man in turn.

'Is that clear?'

They all nodded.

'When you see us leave the bank,' Jesse went on, 'you leave town the same way you came in. There's no orga.nized law in Northfield, so it'll take 'em a while to get a posse together. Ride south to

Willow Creek, you stay there till me, Charlie and Bob get there. We'll divvy up and head west.

'Me and Frank will ride together, the rest of you split up so's we don't draw attention to ourselves. Now let's get some shuteye, it's gonna be a long day tomorrow.'

★ ★ ★

Jesse being spotted in Mankato by pure chance was just one example of a situation you couldn't plan for, and when that happened, he had the sense to cut and run. Jesse and Frank's planning had always been meticulous: trying to cover any eventuality. Of course, it wasn't always perfect, but both brothers tried to expect the unexpected. There'd be other banks and other towns — they were in no hurry as they had plenty of green-backs from previous exploits; despite losing two hundred dollars at the tables in St Paul, they acted as if it was peanuts, and had enough money to buy the best horses, bridles, saddles and bits available.

At the general store, they loaded up with vittles and left town, heading north.

★ ★ ★

Reuben followed his nose to JG Jeft's restaurant. The aroma of steak being cooked over a charcoal pit made his mouth water even more than it was already.

Entering the restaurant, Reuben spotted a table in the far corner that was empty. He made for it and sat down where he could see all the restaurant and the entry door.

It paid to be careful when you were a bounty hunter. He was also aware that whoever had tried to kill him could already be in Northfield.

No sooner had he sat down when a portly waiter, Reuben assumed it to be J.G. Jeft himself, flashed a beaming smile, showing a gold front tooth. He wore pin.stripe trousers, a white shirt with a bootlace tie and a bright-red, silk waist-coat that shimmered in the lantern light.

'Good evening to you, sir,' the waiter said. 'What can I interest you in tonight?'

'That steak sure smells good,' Reuben replied.

'Best in the state,' the waiter said. 'How'd you like it cooked?'

'Bloodier the better,' Reuben said, almost dribbling.

'Eggs, gravy and taters?' the waiter asked.

'You bet,' Reuben said, 'and plenty of coffee.'

'Be right with you,' the waiter said and hurried off to the kitchen.

Reuben leaned back in his chair and glanced around the restaurant. Three tables were occupied, all by what Reuben thought were husband and wife.

For a moment he envied them, sighed, then took out his makings and rolled a cigarette. *Maybe one day*, he thought to himself.

'One ribeye, two eggs and taters,' the waiter said, a beaming smile on his face.

'Coffee'll be right here.'

The steak was so big it overlapped the plate, two over-easy eggs on top and mashed potato in every available space on the plate.

'Sure is a handsome steak,' Reuben said, already cutting into the meat.

'Enjoy,' the waiter said, and scurried back to the kitchen.

Reuben's mouth was too busy chomping to reply.

Two minutes later the waiter returned with a pot of steaming coffee and a ceramic mug. 'How's the steak?' he asked.

'Best I ever had,' Reuben enthused. 'Sure is a quiet town you got here.'

'That's the way we like it, never any bother in Northfield. Shall I pour some coffee?'

'No, it's OK, I'll have the coffee when I've finished the steak,' Reuben answered.

'As you wish, sir,' the waiter almost gave a bow.

'I ain't no "sir". Name's Reuben.'

'Well — Reuben — most folks call me

JG. Pleasure to meet you.'

Reuben was sipping coffee thinking life couldn't get much better. 'A mighty fine meal,' he said, feeling full and satisfied.

'Got some apple pie, if'n you can take it,' JG said.

'Couldn't eat another thing, but I'll bear that in mind next time I'm in.'

'That'll be two dollars and fifty cents,' JG said as he cleared the table.

'Worth every cent, too,' Reuben said and laid three dollars on the table. 'Be seeing you.'

'Sleep well,' JG said as he scooped up the money and headed back to the kitchen.

Little did Reuben know that this night would be his last peaceful one for many weeks.

7

It was a mild September morning that greeted the James Younger gang as they rode at a leisurely pace towards Northfield.

Dressed in linen dusters traditionally worn by cattlemen, the dusters also covered their weapons so to all appearances they were simply cowpokes.

Jesse rode his white-legged sorrel and Charlie Pitts and Bob Younger were mounted on handsome bays. These three were the first to reach Northfield and, reining in, the men dismounted in Mill Square at the foot of the iron bridge that spanned Cannon River.

Jesse took a careful look at the surroundings, making sure that Chadwell and Younger had not overlooked any potential hazards. Satisfied that all was peaceful and that Chadwell's report had been accurate, they mounted up.

'We got time for some chow,' Jesse

said, and headed towards J.G. Jeft's restaurant across the bridge.

JG was wary of the three cowpokes; not his usual jovial self, he didn't know why, but there was something about the three men that made him want them to leave as soon as possible.

'What can I do for you, gents?' JG asked.

Jesse answered for them all: 'Ham and four eggs over easy, that's four eggs each. You got any pie?'

'Sure have, finest apple pie there is,' JG said.

'Then three pies and two pots of coffee,' Jesse ordered.

'Coming right up,' JG said, and hurried back to the kitchen.

Within minutes, the coffee and mugs were served and, no more than five minutes later, the three plates of eggs and ham, along with chunks of fresh bread, were taken to the table.

The three men grabbed their cutlery and began eating. 'Enjoy,' JG said and was only answered with grunts, so he beat a hasty retreat to the relative safety of his kitchen.

The men ate at a leisurely pace, not seeming in much of a hurry. JG kept his eye on them, ready to clear the table and serve up the apple pie as soon as the men had finished.

And finish they did.

JG tried not to show his nervousness, but the sheen of sweat that covered his face was noticed by the ever-astute Jesse.

'You seem a tad uneasy there, friend,' he said to JG.

With slightly trembling hands, JG was in the process of clearing the table. He stopped and gave a weak smile. 'No, no, not at all. It's hot in the kitchen is all.'

Jesse stared hard at the man, but didn't comment further.

JG disappeared and returned almost immediately with the apple pie and a jug of fresh custard. He hastily set them down on the table and said: 'Anything else I can get you, gents?'

'A spoon would be handy,' Charlie said and laughed.

If the ground could have opened and swallowed JG, he would have said thank you!

'So sorry, gents, I'll get them straight away.' He almost ran back to the kitchen returning with the implements. 'Pie's on the house,' he said in a placatory manner.

'Mighty neighbourly,' Charlie said, spooning a chunk of pie and custard into his mouth.

It took the three less than four minutes to clean the plates, then Jesse stood, threw some folding money on the table and, without a word, headed towards the door. He stopped and checked his Hunter.

'Five minutes to go,' was all he said and was joined by Charlie and Bob at the door.

It was a good job they didn't see the relief on JG's face.

★ ★ ★

Reuben had had the best sleep in a long time. Waking at noon, something he hadn't done in years, he stretched and got out of bed.

He pulled the drapes open and looked out onto the alleyway that led to the main street of Northfield.

He was surprised at the amount of activity. The street was teeming with wagons, carts, horsemen and people walking from store to store. Reuben was not used to town living and felt more comfortable out on the range. Nevertheless, it was a peaceful scene, people smiling at friends and acquaintances as they went about their chores.

Reuben washed, sand still encrusted in parts of his hair. Taking his time to dress he made sure his gun was loaded — just in case — and the safety catch was on. Pulling on his Stetson, he made his way to the main street and breathed deeply of the warm air. He walked across the street and looked in some of the stores' windows, amazed at the variety of goods on display. Then he thought of JG Jeft's restaurant; he was ready to eat, maybe another steak. He never got that far.

* * *

At exactly 2 p.m., Jesse James, Charlie Pitts and Bob Younger hitched their mounts outside the First National Bank. The three men stood at the door of the bank for a few moments until they heard the whooping and shooting of three of the gang, clattering over the bridge and through Mill Square and on to Division Street, firing into the air as they rounded the corner. Then, from the opposite end of Division Street, two more members of the gang came in at full gallop, scattering terrified bystanders.

That was the signal for Jesse, Charlie and Bob to enter the bank.

With bandannas covering their faces and weapons drawn, they rushed the counter, shouting at the top of their voices for everyone to put their hands up.

The cashier, Mr Heywood, and the

two clerks, Bunker and Wilcox, looked on horrified as they saw the three men jumping up onto the counter, pistols in their hands.

Heywood was the first to react; he ran towards the vault, but Charlie beat him to it but still Heywood tried to slam the vault door closed to trap Pitts inside. Jesse got there just in time to stop him.

Jesse then noticed the safe inside the vault. 'Open it up,' he ordered.

'I can't,' Heywood almost cried, 'it's on a time lock.'

'That's a damned lie,' Jesse yelled at the man and pistol-whipped him to the floor.

On the other side of the bank, Bob Younger ordered the two clerks to their knees and demanded to know where the cash drawer was. It was Bunker who pointed to the top drawer of the counter.

As Younger rummaged through the coins and loose notes, Bunker made a run for it, aiming for the back door. Charlie Pitts saw him try for it and loosed off a shot.

He missed, but ran forwards and fired again, this time winging Bunker as he tried to escape to the back alley.

If things were not going well inside the bank, they were even worse outside.

Far from it being, as Charlie Pitts had thought, 'Easy as taking candy from a baby', it seemed the townsfolk of North-field weren't a pushover after all.

The five gang members keeping watch outside the bank were under siege.

Despite the lack of weaponry, people had commandeered what handguns and rifles were available in the two hardware stores and were putting up a stiff fight.

Reuben Chisholm, as surprised as anyone, had dived for cover as three of the gang had ridden through, yelling and screaming and firing their guns into the air. All around him panic ensued: screams of women and children as they scurried out of the path of the galloping riders, men yelling, wondering what in hell was going on, and across the square, a horse bolted, towing a small buggy.

At first, most people thought they

were just drunk cow.pokes and would ride straight through town. It didn't take long for them to realize that was not the case.

* * *

They didn't ride on. They reined in outside the bank, weapons drawn, guarding the entrance.

There was an unnatural silence as the townsfolk realized what was going down. The James-Younger gang outside the bank were getting nervous, their mounts jittery.

Then from inside the bank a shot was fired.

* * *

Suddenly, people were running everywhere taking cover and then the shooting started.

Reuben, Colt already drawn, took aim at the riders as a fusillade of shots began to echo throughout the square. Elias

Stacy, a shopkeeper, ran to Division Street and took aim at Clell Miller, but in his haste to grab a weapon, he'd loaded it with bird shot. The blast knocked Miller off his horse, his face taking most of the shot and was bleeding profusely, yet he managed to remount, despite the heavy fall, and charged towards Stacy.

It seemed that Stacy's time was up.

8

Inside the bank, Jesse was getting more and more angry and frustrated. Nothing was going to plan and so far, all they had to show for their efforts were a few measly dollars, and it seemed that was all they were going to get.

'Let's get outta here, pronto,' he called to Charlie and Bob.

'What about the safe?' Charlie said.

'Ain't no way we can get into that sonuver,' Jesse said. 'Best quit and vamoose.'

The three men made for the front door of the bank, then Jesse stopped, his anger overriding every thought in his head. He looked down at the still-dazed cashier, and without a thought, put his Colt to the man's temple and blew his brains out. He had to vent his anger on some.thing, and in this case, someone!

Little did he know then what the outcome of that single shot would be.

It didn't take Jesse long to find out, though.

As they reached the door of the bank, it seemed the whole of Northfield was just one loud explosion of rifle, scatter-gun and pistol fire.

For the first time in his life, Jesse stood stock-still in both surprise and horror. He watched as Clell got a face-full of buckshot that knocked him off his mount, then remount and charge towards the shooter. What he didn't expect was what happened next.

Henry Wheeler, a medical student on vacation from the University of Michigan, was in his father's drugstore when the shooting started. He suddenly remembered the old army carbine that he hoped was still in the baggage room of the Dampier House next door.

His luck was in as the carbine was still there. He grabbed it and dashed to an upstairs front room.

He had a clear view of Miller charging down on the helpless Stacy. Breathing deeply then holding his breath, Henry brought up the carbine, sighted down the barrel and gently squeezed the trigger.

Clell Miller was knocked back with such force that he hit the dirt twenty feet from his horse. Cole Younger was the first to reach him. He dismounted and yelled: 'Clell! You OK?'

Miller tried to get up, but he couldn't, and wouldn't do again. He rolled over and died on the spot.

Younger, showing no sign of emotion at all, took off Clell's cartridge belt and pistols and got back on his horse.

The air was thick with gun-smoke, the acrid fumes almost reaching choking level; the sound of the various weapons was deafening and the thundering sound of hoofs as the outlaws tried every means to escape. It was like a scene straight out of hell.

Amidst the chaos, a newly-arrived Swedish immigrant was making his way down Division Street towards the bank. Despite frantic calls for him to get out the road he kept walking. No one knew the man could speak no English.

And now, he never would. A single slug took out the back of his skull; it seemed that his head just exploded, and the man crumpled to the ground.

The townsmen were more organized now. The frenzied shooting was deliberate and careful. Stacy had run up an outside staircase at the corner of the Scriver Block, clambered inside and, from a window facing Division Street, continued to blast away with his bird shot at the robbers.

The hardware merchant, Manning, levelled his Remington repeating rifle and took careful aim at Bill Chadwell as he rode down the street. The bullet went straight through his heart and Chadwell was catapulted from the saddle. He was dead before he hit the ground.

Manning took aim again, this time hitting Cole Younger in the shoulder.

The townsfolk got better coordinated as more and more people joined in the fight, so the outlaws' chances of escaping grew slimmer.

Frank James was hit in the leg, and

Jim Younger in the face, blood gushing uncontrollably from his mouth. Yet the gang continued to ride up and down the street shooting at anything that moved and through doors and windows.

Suddenly, Bob Younger leapt from his horse and used it as a shield then aimed his six-gun at Manning who was still on the Scriver Block stairway. But Manning fired first, hitting the bay in the neck. Younger managed to dodge the falling horse and sought shelter behind a stack of boxes.

He didn't realize that Henry Wheeler could see him clearly from the upstairs window of the Dampier House. Wheeler fired and caught Bob Younger in the right thigh.

Reuben couldn't be sure if he'd hit anyone or not. In the confusion, noise and the number of weapons being fired, it was hard to tell, but he did think he'd caught Frank James.

It was the Younger Brothers that Reuben was after. He was sure that both Clarke and Adams were in cahoots with them back in the Quantrill days. Frank and Jesse were an obvious bonus, not that he had any hopes now of claiming bounty on any of them as it seemed that every man in Northfield had participated in foiling the bank raid by the James-Younger gang.

There came a moment of silence, a silence that was as deafening as the gunfire had been.

In that few seconds of quiet, a voice rang out.

'We're beat! Let's get outta here!'

At that moment, Bob Younger limped into the middle of the street and called out: 'Hold on, don't leave me, I'm shot!'

Cole Younger turned his mount and headed towards his brother. At that moment another Northfield man let loose with a scattergun and the buckshot shattered Bob's right elbow. Nevertheless, Cole managed to lift his brother onto his horse and together they raced off after the rest of the gang, the metal-shod hoofs rattling as they crossed the Cannon River bridge.

9

In just over twenty minutes, the fighting in Northfield came to an abrupt halt.

Gradually, people began to emerge from their homes, shops and offices to survey the scene. Bodies littered the street, along with a dead horse.

Of the eight gang members, six had escaped alive, albeit with four of them wounded. Bill Chadwell and Clell Miller were dead, as were three townsmen.

Reuben was one of the first to hit the main street. He checked the two dead outlaws, he didn't want any unwel.come surprises. He'd seen men play possum too many times to take anything for granted. Satisfied they were dead, Reuben holstered his gun, tilted his Stetson back, wiped his brow with a bandanna and took a deep breath.

Seasoned as he was, the full horror of that twenty minutes sent a cold shiver down his spine.

But it wasn't over yet — not by a long shot.

The two men he was after were not among the dead.

Reuben glanced around the town square, the shattered windows and bullet-hole riddled buildings; the smell of black powder still thick in the air and small groups of people just standing and staring, shock written all over their faces.

Down by the Cannon River bridge, Reuben saw a group of five or six men having an animated discussion. They all wore long, black, frock-coats, string ties and bowler hats. *Town elders*, Reuben thought, *God save us from committees*.

Reuben edged closer, trying to hear the discussion. Some were suggesting a posse should be formed straight away; others that the gang would get their comeuppance soon enough and there was no point in putting any more lives at risk.

But the town elders had made a quick decision to call the Pinkerton Agency to get help.

It was also decided to send telegrams to alert the whole state, and soon hundreds of Minnesotans set out to finish the job Northfield had started.

A posse was quickly formed, and they set off after the remaining members of the gang.

Reuben immediately ran to the livery, saddled up and rode hell for leather.

The tracks were fresh and easy to follow. He still had three Younger brothers to capture — dead or alive. Four riders had headed north, the other two south. Reuben decided to head north.

He wasn't a hundred per cent sure they were the men who'd killed his wife, but he was sure that of the six riders that had escaped, he'd find them, and the Youngers had a huge bounty on their heads, but more importantly, they might know the identity of the two men he wanted.

Reuben rode on for another twenty minutes, then reined in sharply.

The tracks split.

Dismounting, Reuben knelt and studied the hoof prints in the soft earth. A tracker of long experience, it didn't take him long to see that the riders had separated. Three had taken the right-hand trail and one the left. Reuben made a quick decision to follow the left-hand trail.

The trail was still easy to follow. The rain had softened the earth, making it impossible to hide the tracks of a galloping horse.

What Reuben didn't know was that he, too, was being trailed.

The two other riders had a change of heart, thinking if the Youngers had headed north, then they should too.

Bypassing Northfield, they quickly joined the northern trail and it didn't take them long to discover five sets of hoof prints in the soft earth.

10

The tracks Reuben was following had ceased to show a galloping horse. It was obvious the rider he was chasing felt safe and had slowed his animal down so as not to tire it too much.

Reuben reined in slightly, he didn't want the rider ahead to see or hear him — yet.

After another ten minutes, Reuben caught sight of a small dust cloud on the trail ahead. The sun was begin.ning to dry the damp earth. He was near.

He slowed down more and kept the dust cloud in view, hoping the rider didn't turn around and see him.

Meanwhile, the three riders were rapidly catching up. They had already reached the fork in the trail and, halting, one of the men dismounted and studied the ground.

'Three headed right, the other one left,' he said.

'I reckon whoever is trailing the Youngers, went left.'

He remounted, and the three men set off down the left-hand trail.

By now, Reuben was down to a gentle trot as he kept pace with the man he was chasing. He knew that the man was riding towards a secret hideaway, probably pre-arranged. He also assumed the other Younger brother would join him there by a different route.

Cunning, but not *that* cunning.

The three riders could see their quarry, he was within rifle shot, but shooting from a galloping horse and hitting the target was only a slim chance. They waited till they got nearer, reined in, and one of the men took aim.

Although he didn't have the benefit of the scope that sat atop Reuben's Winchester, he was a good shot.

A split second after he heard the crack of the rifle shot, Reuben was thrown from his horse as the slug hit him high on the left shoulder.

The fall, rather than the slug, rendered

him unconscious.

'Who the hell is he?' asked one of the men.

'Never seen him afore,' came an answer.

'Git him tied up, we'll take him with us, find out who he is.'

★ ★ ★

Slowly, Reuben regained consciousness. He could see nothing.

At first he thought he'd been blind-folded but could feel nothing on his face. Then he realized he was in a dark room. Everything was just black, even the window had been boarded up.

He tried to sit up, but he'd been hog-tied. His hands behind his back and the rope extended to his ankles, he was tied to a rickety chair and gagged. *Who the hell were these men*, he thought to himself. They must be chancers. Out to get whatever they could, by fair means or foul.

Reuben gathered his thoughts together. There must be some way of getting out of this mess.

He tried pulling on the ropes, but they were tight, too tight. His fingers and feet were beginning to feel numb.

There was no way he could use his throwing knife this time, he tried to move his legs to see if he could feel it, but his legs couldn't or wouldn't move.

Straining as hard as he could, the pain in his left shoulder agonizing, he began to rock the chair from side to side. Eventually he fell sideways as the chair collapsed. He landed heavily on his bad shoulder. It took all his strength not to scream out in pain.

Stretching as far as he could, the pain intense in his left shoulder, he managed to slide free the rope that bound his hands to the now broken chair.

Reuben relaxed, sweat seeming to seep out of every pore in his body and his breathing laboured from the exertion. When he felt he was ready, he started to pull at the slackened ropes, now free of the chair; gradually, his right hand was free enough to tackle the left hand that was still tied tightly. He relaxed again, breathing deeply, conserving his energy and fighting the intense pain as if his life depended on it. He grinned: his life did depend on it, he was sure of that.

Now came the hard part.

With both hands now free of the ropes he still had his left arm trapped under his body, he tried to roll on to his back and free his arm so he could tackle the ropes that bound his legs to the chair.

Looking down, Reuben saw that not only had his boots been stolen, but his knife as well. There was no easy way out this time. He would have to unpick the knots. From its thickness, Reuben knew it was a lariat, tougher than other ropes, and it was tightly bound.

He began to pick at the nearest knot, breaking his fin.gernails as he fought the tough hemp, his wrists on fire with pain from the effort. He wasn't sure if the moisture he felt dripping from his fingers was sweat or blood.

He rather thought it was the latter.

It seemed to take hours before the last

strand began to loosen and he felt blood course through his right leg and he had to rest. Pins and needles took hold, as the blood rushed eagerly into his leg. The pain in his hands was excruciating but he had to ignore it as best he could as he still had his left leg to free.

Taking deep breaths, Reuben set about the last knot. He tried to slide the rope down the chair leg, but a broken strut halted its progress. There was no alternative other than to untie the knot.

Despite the pain in his hands, he wriggled and teased at the knot until, at long last, it became looser. Again, blood began to reach his lower leg and he had to stop and rest.

One final attack and he was free — of the ropes at least.

Reuben lay flat on his back, getting both his breath and strength back. At length the pins and needles abated and he felt strong enough to stand. The room was as black as hell, but there was a sliver of light to his left, which he assumed came from an ill-fitting door.

He was right. But the door was locked.

Mustering what he thought would be his last ounce of strength for a while, he used his good shoulder to charge at the door.

It was flimsier than he'd anticipated and gave way easily, sending Reuben flying through the air to land heavily in the hard-packed door. Bright sunshine flooded his eyes, temporarily blinding him.

When he got used to the light, he looked back inside.

In one corner was a table. No gun this time; they'd obviously learned a lesson.

These guys were either amateurs or they were convinced he'd never be able to escape.

They had left his Stetson, so he retrieved it and scanned the terrain.

He saw and heard nothing.

Moving around the shack, he saw nothing.

His horse had gone this time, too.

But lying in the dirt, he spotted his war-bag and beside it, his Winchester.

It didn't make sense. Why had they left those two items? Now he was armed. The war-bag was closed, so he knew, as he opened it up, that his stash of ammo was still there.

On foot, with no boots, he stood little chance of finding the thieves. He also stood little chance of surviving!

As he sat and thought of what to do next, he heard distant hoof beats heading his way.

Listening closely, he reckoned four horses.

Grabbing his rifle, he lay on the ground behind the shack. The hoof beats stopped abruptly.

Damn! he thought. He'd left the door to the shack lying on the ground. The element of surprise was lost.

Removing his Stetson, Reuben took a quick look out front. There were four riders, but from this distance, he couldn't recognize them.

Slowly, the four men began to walk their animals towards the cabin.

When they were no more than forty

feet from the shack, they halted again and one of the men lifted out his Winchester and dismounted, walking slowly towards the building.

Reuben recognized the man immediately, He was one of the ex-Quantrill raiders and was the spitting image of the Wanted poster he had stared at many times. It was 'Bloody' Bill Anderson, probably the most dangerous of the Quantrill gang who had survived the last battle William Quantrill had fought.

So it was him in particular that they were after. Anderson has obviously remembered him from the failed bank robbery. They hadn't killed him because they wanted a slow death for him.

It all became clear now.

Moving slowly to his right, Reuben levelled his Winchester. His head and right shoulder was exposed as he sighted on the man walking towards the shack.

He ignored the pain in his left shoulder and kept the Winchester steady. He aimed for the man's right thigh. No way was he going to make his death quick.

He planned on taking him back to Northfield where he would be tried and hopefully hanged.

Holding his breath, Reuben gently squeezed the trigger.

The thunder from the rifle was shattering, the previous silence making it sound like a thunder-clap.

It was followed by a high-pitched scream as Anderson fell to the dirt, clutching his right leg.

The other three riders pulled rein and galloped off in the direction of Madelia, Minnesota. Try as he might, Reuben couldn't see the men's faces. But he took aim and took another of them out.

Now he had two horses. His hopes rose that he'd survive after all.

When the remaining two riders were just a distant dust cloud, Reuben struggled to his feet, and entered the shack, retrieving the ropes that had bound him.

Holding his rifle level, he slowly approached the stricken man who was, by now, groaning rather than screaming.

But Reuben was careful. He hadn't

lived this long to be fooled by an injured man who might reach for his gun.

Anderson made no movement as Reuben stood over him.

'Go ahead, finish me off,' Anderson said.

'No way,' Reuben replied. 'I'm taking you in to face trial and hang. There ain't no easy death for you,' Reuben added.

Reuben knelt and removed the man's hand gun, then kicked his Winchester to one side. He felt the man's boots, but there was no hidden knife.

Using a small piece of the rope, Reuben placed a crude tourniquet around the man's thigh above the wound. There wasn't much bleeding, so he figured he hadn't hit an artery. He'd survive the journey.

He then tied the man's hands — tightly.

'You got a choice,' Reuben said. 'Sit a saddle, or I'll tie you across your horse. You choose.

'I'll ride,' Anderson replied.

Reuben brought the man's animal around to his left side.

'Put your left foot into the stirrup, I'll hold your right leg and lift it over,' Reuben said.

Anderson complied.

Reuben fetched his own horse from the back of the shack and tied a rope from his pommel to Anderson's. He picked up Anderson's Colt and Winchester, and stored them in his saddlebags, they then headed back to Northfield.

11

Cole, Bob and Jim Younger were indeed heading for Madelia, where they would hide out until the dust settled.

They didn't realize the dust *wouldn't* settle.

* * *

Reuben and Anderson had an uneventful journey back to Northfield, arriving around four in the afternoon.

They were immediately surrounded by the townsfolk, who recognized Anderson and hauled him from his horse, and marched him to the jail block.

The doctor was summoned, and he saw to the wounded leg. He didn't do the best of jobs, leaving the slug in his leg, but at least the bleeding had stopped, so he'd last until he hanged.

Reuben was feted by the citizens of Northfield, the pats on his back and offers of free drinks and room and board were tempting. But all Reuben wanted was something to eat and his horse seen to.

This was taken care of immediately. While he ate a bloody steak, with gravy and potatoes, his horse was fed and watered and well groomed, his mane shining in the late afternoon sun.

JG Jeft, the owner of the restaurant, walked across to Reuben, who was just finishing the last of his coffee.

'Everything to your satisfaction, Mr Chisholm?' he asked.

'Finest steak I ever had,' Reuben replied. 'Any news on the bank robbery?'

Jeft laughed. 'Well, we killed two of them, and wounded two of the Younger boys. Jesse and his brother managed to escape uninjured. Sadly, two of the townsfolk were killed: Joseph Heywood, a bank teller, and a new arrival from someplace called Europe, Sweden, I think.'

'How much money did they get?' Reuben asked.

This time, Jeft laughed so hard he

almost fell over, his big belly shaking like a huge jelly.

'They got just over two dollars,' he said, tears rolling down his fat cheeks.

Reuben didn't laugh. 'So, four dead. Fifty cents each.'

That halted Jeft's laughter.

'Sorry,' Jeft said, hanging his head. 'I never thought of it that way.'

'How much do I owe you?' Reuben asked.

'Not a cent. Dinner's on the house. Your money won't be accepted while you're in Northfield. A thank you for your help in bringing in that murdering scumbag,' Jeft said, clearing the table.

' 'Preciate that, Mr Jeft. Now I need a tub and some sleep. Be seeing you,' Reuben left the restaurant and crossed the square to the Dampier Hotel. He'd need a second night there.

Henry Potter gave a huge smile as Reuben entered the lobby.

'Welcome back, Mr Chisholm. I'm sure the whole town owes you a great debt. We certainly applaud your bravery,'

Potter gushed.

'The Pinkertons have killed or wounded most of the gang, 'cept Frank an' Jesse. They reckon they headed towards the Dakotas. But they'll get their comeuppance. They just don't accept the war is over.'

'Well, that's good news. Them Pinkerton fellas sure do work fast,' Reuben said. Then, changing the subject, Reuben said, 'I need the room for another night, and a hot tub, Mr Potter. If that's possible?' Reuben asked. 'And thank you for your kindly comments.'

'My pleasure, Mr Chisholm. Your room is ready, and I'll get the house staff to sort the tub out right away.'

Reuben reached into his vest pocket and handed over some money.

'No need, Mr Chisholm, it's on the house as a thank you,' Potter said, holding up hands palms forward. 'As is breakfast in the morning. Any time between eight and ten.'

'Mighty gracious of you, Mr Potter,' Reuben replied as he made his way upstairs on weary legs. It had been a long and harrowing day.

But it wasn't over yet.

12

Henry Moon, long-time partner of Bloody Bill Anderson, had overheard a conversation in a saloon, about the failed bank raid in Northfield.

As he listened he heard the name Anderson!

Moon moved from the bar and stood in front of the two men. 'Buy you a drink, fellas? I'd like to know what you heard about the Northfield bank robbery.' Moon smiled at the two men who were completely unaware of the identity of the man speaking to them.

'Sure thing, mister, beer would be fine.' They didn't even ask his name.

Moon returned to the table with the beers and sat opposite the two men.

'What we heard is that the James-Younger gang tried to hold up the First National Bank in Northfield. It didn't go down too well,' one of the men began.

'Seems two of the gang were killed

outright, and Cole and Jim Younger were wounded, but managed to escape, as did Jesse and his brother Frank, along with two others. Bill Anderson was one, the other unknown,' the second man said.

'They get away with much?' Moon asked.

Both men laughed. 'Hell no, a little over two dollars.'

Henry laughed too. But not with his eyes.

'Thanks, fellas. Enjoy your beers,' Henry said, and
stood to leave the saloon.

'That ain't the end of it,' one of them said.

'Well?' Henry asked.

'Seems some fella by the name of Chisholm went after them and caught up with Anderson. Took him back to Northfield with a slug in his leg. He's in the jailhouse, waiting for the trial. Ain't no doubt he'll hang for sure.'

'Thanks again, fellas,' Henry said and left the saloon.

Dusk was falling fast as Henry was

leaving, soon it would be dark. There was no moon in sight as the thick, black clouds scudded across the sky. He'd have to head to Northfield come first light.

Tonight, he would sleep under the stars.

Reuben checked into his room and gave a soft whistle. It was nothing like he'd ever seen before.

A huge bedroom with a double bed. Bedside tables on either side with oil lamps already lit, and a bottle of the finest Scotch whisky and a crystal tumbler stood on a highly polished oak table, surrounded by four straight-back chairs.

In the right-hand corner, double opening windows led out onto a small balcony. There was a huge sofa with cushions scattered all over it.

Next to the sofa was another door. Reuben opened it carefully, in case it was someone else's room. But it wasn't.

If Reuben was surprised by the quality

of his room, he was astounded to find a tub and wash basin and a bucket with a lid on it, the toilet, he presumed. A pitcher and jug stood on a chest of drawers, the water clean.

Reuben became instantly alert as a knock on his door sounded louder because of the silence.

He drew his Colt and moved towards the door, standing to one side. He didn't want a bullet fired through the door.

'Who's there?' he asked.

'Complimentary coffee, sir,' came the reply.

'Just leave it on the floor out there,' Reuben said.

'As you wish, sir.'

Reuben heard the contents of the tray rattle as it was placed on the carpeted hallway floor. Then the soft footfalls of the departing waiter.

Reuben waited for five minutes before slowly opening the door, his Colt cocked.

On the floor was a silver tray with a coffee pot, cup and saucer, milk and a bowl of sugar. Next to these was a plate of cookies.

Reuben holstered his gun and bent down to pick up the tray. As he stood, a shot rang out. He felt the air rush past him as the bullet thudded harmlessly into the wall facing Main Street.

Without dropping the tray, Reuben kicked the door shut and placed the tray on one of the bedside tables.

Then he took his side-iron out once more and went back to the door. His ear pressed against the wall, listening.

All was silent.

Slowly, he opened the door once more and took a quick look down the hallway, his finger putting pressure on the trigger, ready to shoot if anyone was still there.

The hallway, around thirty yards long, was empty.

Slowly, Reuben edged his way towards the end of the hallway. When he reached the corner, he halted, listening intently.

He heard nothing.

Crouching, he peered around the corner, but the second hallway was also empty. Reuben headed for the head of the stairs leading to the lobby.

Leaning over the banister, Reuben could see the body of the hotel owner, Henry Potter, lying beside the front desk.

Reuben pulled back the hammer on his Colt and slowly descended the stairs.

Scanning the lobby area, Reuben made sure there was no one in sight. It seemed empty.

Moving towards Potter's unmoving body, he knelt and felt for a pulse.

The man was alive; seems he was cold-cocked, judging by the lump on the back of his head.

Then Reuben heard a noise from somewhere near the lobby. He dragged Potter behind the lobby desk. Reuben kept his head low, just high enough to peer over the desk.

A shot rang out, but Reuben's reactions were lightning fast. The bullet lodged into the wood of the desk, sending deadly splinters of wood skywards.

Reuben didn't waste any time. In the micro second that it took for the bullet to reach the desk, he'd seen the muzzle flash. He lifted his Colt and fired in the general direction.

Another shot rang out, hitting almost the same place as the first. Reuben loosed off three quick shots, and on the third, heard a deep groan.

He'd made a hit.

Reuben crawled to the far side of the lobby desk, peered cautiously to his right, and saw a body.

Meanwhile, Henry Potter began to come to. Reuben rushed to his side.

'Keep down, there might be more than one gunman,' he whispered to Potter.

They waited another five minutes before Reuben stood up. The body hadn't moved and there'd been no more shots.

The man was dead. Reuben stared at the man's face, but didn't have a Wanted poster on him and had no idea who he was.

13

As he knelt by the body, Henry Potter stood, holding his head, wondering what the hell had gone on. At the same time, townsfolk entered the hotel and stood looking at Reuben, not quite knowing what to make of what they saw.

It was Henry Potter who spoke first.

'I got cold-cocked,' he said. 'But Mr Chisholm there saved my life.' Everyone moved closer to the body. 'Anybody recognize him?' Reuben asked. He was met by a shaking of heads, then one man stepped forward. 'He was one of the bank robbers,' he said. 'I saw him as clear as day.' 'Anyone know his name?' Reuben asked. No one answered. 'What the hell he come back here for?' Potter asked. 'He was trying to kill me,' Reuben replied. 'Why? I have no idea.'

* * *

Henry Moon rose at the same time that the sun tipped over the distant mountains. He made coffee, but did not eat.

Northfield was a good four-hour ride and he was eager to get going. No way was he going to let Anderson hang.

Draining his coffee mug, he packed his gear into his war bag, saddled up and set off.

The ride to Northfield was uneventful, and he knew he'd have a week at most to bust Anderson from jail. When he was around an hour from the town, he reined in and found a sheltered spot where he'd wait till nightfall. Then he'd make his move.

Again, he built a small fire, got the coffee brewing and slung some fat-back bacon and beans into a pan, then unsaddled and fed and watered his horse, before lying back and resting his head on the hard, Western saddle.

It was the smell of the bacon and coffee that woke him from a shallow sleep. He ate from the pan and sipped at the coffee between mouthfuls.

Feeling refreshed, Moon looked to the sky. In the west, the sun was beginning to lower and he knew that soon it would be dark, but he'd have to wait until at least mid.night before he made his move.

He'd planned in his head what he was going to do. He knew the layout of Northfield pretty well. He knew exactly where the livery stable was, and knew instinctively that Anderson's horse would be stabled there, to be sold, no doubt, when they'd hanged him.

The jail was small and unguarded and at midnight, the folks of Northfield would be sound asleep.

His own horse was ground-hitched and chewing contentedly, so Moon lay back down and slept some more.

It would be a long night.

* * *

Reuben had a long and relaxing soak in the tub; a glass of champagne in one hand and a cigar in the either. He had never felt so good in his life.

Reluctantly, he stood up and reached for a towel and dried himself off. Hanging on the back of the door was a dressing gown. *The height of luxury*, he thought.

Standing by the window, cigar in hand, he watched as darkness fell and the stores began closing for the night. Shutters were drawn, and oil lamps extinguished.

He watched as the lamp man walked down Main Street, lighting the street lamps that would burn till daybreak, then return to snuff them out and refill them with oil. His job for the day until nightfall came around again.

Reuben stubbed out his cigar, removed the dressing gown and slipped on his long Johns, checked his Colts and hung the gun-belt on the bed post, placing one gun under his pillow before climbing into bed.

The sheets were crisp and clean, and the bed cover as soft as down.

He was in heaven and, within minutes, was asleep.

★   ★   ★

Henry Moon woke with a start. The sound of a distant coyote's howl echoed through the air. The fire had burned itself out and Moon shivered. Taking out his Huntsman pocket watch, he squinted at the timepiece.

It was 11.30p.m. Time to get ready, but first he must have some coffee; it might be a while before he would have another opportunity to relax. He relit the fire and soon had the coffee pot warming up.

The coyote's howl was joined by another, then another. Moon's horse began stomping his hoofs on the ground, clearly spooked. Moon reached into his saddlebag and filled his hat with some oats and barley mix and the horse calmed down as it ate.

Moon made sure the fire was completely out, pouring cold coffee on it and kicking sand over its remains. He rolled up the bedroll in his tarp, then saddled up, tying the tarp securely, fitting the bridle and bit, and finally hitching his war bag on his pommel and saddlebags across the animal's rump.

Making sure he'd left no sign, he headed off at a walk towards Northfield.

* * *

The Pinkerton Agents seemed to be everywhere and, in some cases, were as dangerous as the James-Younger gang. They tried every trick in the book to capture or kill — preferably kill — all the surviving gang members.

Most of the gang had headed for Madelia, where they hoped they'd be safe before moving further afield.

Meanwhile, Frank and Jesse had split from the rest of the gang and escaped to Missouri, safe for the time being.

* * *

Henry Moon reached the outskirts of Northfield at 12.15 a.m. He avoided the lit main street and used the dark alleyways to make his way to the stables.

Arriving at the rear entrance of the livery, Moon dismounted and tied his horse to a corral post. He pulled a Bowie knife from the sheath at his hip and peered through the plank door.

One oil-lamp gave a dull, yellow light to the interior. Moon figured it was either for the old-timer who might be sleeping there, or for the benefit of the horses.

Moon reckoned on the latter.

He leaned gently on the door — it wasn't even locked, so maybe the livery-man was asleep inside. He pushed at the door an inch at a time. The metal hinges creaked and in the silence of the night the horses inside the livery became jittery.

Moon added more pressure to the door, so it moved a foot this time, and the hinges didn't squeak. He slipped inside.

He spotted Anderson's horse straight away, the saddle resting on the barrier that separated the stalls.

Then he heard the snoring.

Turning, Moon saw the old-timer asleep on a pile of hay, a half-empty bottle of bourbon still gripped in his right hand.

Moon smiled as he walked towards the sleeping man. His Bowie knife slid between the ribs, puncturing the heart. The livery man died without even knowing it.

He carefully cleaned the bloody knife on the dead man's shirt before returning it to its sheath.

Grabbing hold of the old man's legs, he hauled him onto the pile of hay and covered the body.

He hunted round the stables and found what he was looking for: a stout rope.

Then, saddling Anderson's horse, he led it out of the stables and, keeping a hold on the reins, mounted his own horse and walked both animals to the rear of the jail and tethered them to a post.

He crept up to the rear of the jail and peered through the first of three cells. There was no glass, just iron bars.

The cell was empty, so he moved to the next, also empty. He edged to the last cell and saw Anderson asleep on a small cot.

Moon looped one end of the rope through the cell bars and pulled so the ends were even. Then he hooked one end of the rope to Anderson's pommel, the other end he tied to his own.

Grabbing the reins of Anderson's horse, he held those of both horses and yanked hard. The animals, taken by surprise, rushed forward, pulling the rope taut and the air was filled with the sound of the cell bars being wrenched from the jail and clattering on the ground.

Hell, thought Moon, *you coulda kicked them out!*

A face, lined with pain, appeared at the window. Moon coiled the rope as he calmed the horses.

'What ya waitin' fer?' called Moon.

'I got a bullet in my leg,' Anderson said. 'I need some help here.'

Henry Moon ambled towards Anderson and gripped him under his arms and pulled. Anderson winced, but using his good leg, managed to help Moon and then dropped to the ground.

Anderson wanted to scream in agony,

128

but gritted his teeth, aware that it would be heard by someone.

Moon pulled him up onto his horse.

'Mount to the left,' Moon said. 'I'll help with your right then we ride and find a doc in the next town north.'

Moon led Anderson out of Northfield by the same route he had entered.

The night was moonless, dark clouds were still scudding across the sky as Anderson and Moon set off at a steady trot which soon slowed to a walk. The last thing either man wanted was a lame mount.

They had been riding for three hours when Anderson reined in.

'I gotta rest awhiles. My leg's hurting something awful. The doc in Northfield didn't bother taking out the slug as they were planning to hang me the next day.'

Moon made no response.

'There's a tree yonder, you can rest up there,' Moon said. 'I'll ride into town and get a doc out here, pronto.'

Helping Anderson down, he leaned him against the tree and mounted up.

'I'll be back as quick as I can,' Moon added, before setting off for town.

Dawn was approaching so Henry Moon was able to travel at a gallop.

It was half an hour later that he saw smoke in the dis.tance.

He dug out his Huntsman and checked the time: it was 5.30 a.m. He'd have to wake the doc, of that he was certain.

He rode into town, which looked like many towns he'd ridden into. Clapboard buildings, a saloon, barber shop, general shop, livery stable and finally, he saw a sign: Duncan Mackay MD.

Dismounting, Moon took out his Colt; he doubted the doc would come willingly, and rapped hard on the door.

'*Goddammit*!' a gruff voice came from inside the doctor's house/surgery. 'What the hell you want at this time o' the day?' he grumbled.

'You gotta take a bullet out o' my pal's leg,' Moon said. 'Well, bring him in then,' Mackay said reluctantly. 'Can't do that. He's an hour's ride away so get your gear together. Now!'

130

'I ain't ridin' out,' the doc said.

'See this?' Moon said as he levelled his Colt. 'Get your gear together!'

The doctor gulped. 'I gotta dress first,' he almost whispered.

'I'll be right behind you,' Moon replied.

After dressing, Moon helped Mackay hitch up his buggy and the two men set off. It wasn't full daylight yet, but as they left town, lights began to be lit as people prepared for their day's labour. Moon didn't notice the twitching of a drape in one of the smaller houses as a woman saw the doctor in his buggy with a man riding a horse, his gun drawn.

* * *

William Clarke and Alexander Adams were a hundred miles south of Northfield when they overheard the news of the failed bank robbery in a saloon.

Like all passed-on stories and rumours, the news grew out of all proportion.

Hundreds were killed. Thousands

of dollars were taken. And the James-Younger gang had escaped, scott.free!

Clarke and Adams could hardly believe their ears.

'Damn!' Clarke muttered. 'We goddamn missed out!'

Adams ignored this remark as he moved closer to the group of men, trying to glean as much information as he could.

He didn't believe for one moment that hundreds were killed. But he wasn't so sure that the amount of money was made up.

''Scuse me fellas,' Adams said, 'where'd you hear this news?'

'Fella in the corner, yonder,' the man pointed to a corner table and a man surrounded by beer, but sitting alone.

Adams didn't say another word but walked back to Clarke, who was downing whiskey like water.

'Hold down on that drinking,' Adams said. 'I'm gonna have a chat with that fella in the corner. He's the one who brought the story into town.'

'What good's that gonna do?' Clarke replied.

'I wanna know what's right and what really happened up there in Northfield. Jesse ain't no fool. He wouldn't try robbing a bank without knowing it was safe to do so. Wait here. I'll be back, and don't drink any more until I do.'

Clarke nodded.

Adams walked across the saloon and stood at the man's table.

'Mind if'n I join you?' Adams asked.

'Sure thing, mister. Help yourself.'

'Mind telling me what really happened up in Northfield?' Adams asked.

'I already tol' what happened,' the old-timer said.

'I know what you told them fellas at the bar, there, that's how come this table is full of free beer.' Adams paused. 'You see my left hand on the table?'

'Yeah. Why?'

'Cos my right hand is holding a pistol aimed at your beer belly,' Adam stated calmly.

The man's jaw dropped, and he slowly

lowered his glass to the table.

Shaking, his voice like a whisper as fear gripped him, he related what had *really* happened in Northfield.

'So the Youngers are badly wounded?'

'Yes, sir. Three other members of the gang were killed outright.'

'Where are they now?' Adams asked.

'Locked in the doc's basement, under guard. They're waitin' for the circuit judge to arrive.'

'And the rest of the gang?' Adams still held his right hand under the table.

'High-tailed it faster than a coyote chasin' a rabbit. Headed north, far as I could figure,' the old-timer said.

'And Frank and Jesse?' Adams asked.

'Oh, they got away all right. Town council got a posse goin' after 'em, but them's city folk. Doubt they'd catch 'em.'

'Enjoy your beer, old man,' Adams said, and left the table.

The old-timer picked up his beer, hands still shaking and managed a big gulp before lighting a small, half-smoked cheroot.

Adams related the true story to Clarke and the two men finished their drinks and left the saloon.

They headed north.

14

Reuben's eyes opened with a start. There was no noise and for a moment or two he wondered where he was.

He reached for his Hunter. It was 11 a.m.

Damn, he thought, *I've missed breakfast!*

He quickly washed and dressed, hoping he'd at least get a coffee or two.

He left the room, locking the door behind him and made his way to the lobby.

The desk clerk immediately guided him to the restau.rant and a pot of coffee appeared as if by magic.

'Good morning, Mr Chisholm. I trust you slept well?'

'I sure did,' Reuben answered.

'Breakfast will be with you in a short while,' the desk clerk told him.

'That's mighty good of you,' Reuben said. 'I thought breakfast finished at ten.'

'Not for you, Mr Chisholm,' the clerk said, and excused himself.

It took ten minutes for the breakfast to arrive — it barely fit on the plate — and five minutes to eat it!

Pouring himself another coffee, Reuben sat back and relaxed. He still had a job to do, but for ten minutes he was at peace with the world until . . . .

'Mr Chisholm! Mr Chisholm!'

A cowboy rushed into the restaurant, quickly removing his bowler hat. 'Mr Chisholm, sir, that Anderson fella has been busted out of jail!'

Reuben almost jumped out of his chair. 'How the hell?'

'Seems someone pulled the bars and most of the rear wall down,' the cowboy informed him.

Reuben grabbed his Stetson and rushed from the restaurant. He wanted to see the site for himself.

At the back of the jail, over a dozen men had gathered, gawping.

Reuben took a brief look at the jail wall and the bars that wouldn't keep a child in and then stepped back, looking for sign.

The ground round the jail had been trampled so he moved further back, looking from side to side.

He spotted two sets of hoof-prints heading north. He ran to the livery and readied his horse.

Mounting up, he slowly walked his horse along the trail, noting Main Street had been avoided. The trail went left and then right, running parallel to Main, but the dirt road was little used at night as it was unlit, so the tracks were easy to follow as they left town, still heading north.

As much as he wanted to find the two men who had killed his wife, he wasn't about to let Anderson get away.

15

The doc reined in his buggy and clambered to the ground, grabbing his medical bag as he approached the stricken man.

The first thing he took out of his bag was a bottle of lau.danum.

'Here, you'll need this,' he said.

Anderson grabbed the bottle and pulled the cork out with his teeth. He didn't say a word as he took a mighty mouthful.

'Hey, careful with that stuff. It's addictive,' the doc said.

'Add — what?' Anderson asked.

'It means you'll need to keep takin' it,' Moon said as if talking to an idiot.

'What, forever?' Anderson asked.

'Right up till it kills you,' Mackay added.

Undeterred, Anderson took another swig at the bottle. The laudanum was having an effect. He felt light-headed and pain free.

'Let's cut the chit-chat. Get that leg fixed, Doc. Pronto!' Moon said.

'Well, let's hope the sewin' on the wound is better than on these jeans, looks like a child did it,' the doctor said.

Anderson looked up at him and said, 'there ain't no sewing on the wound. Sheriff said weren't worth the effort.' Anderson smiled then, his eyes half closed, the effects of the laudanum taking over.

Pulling apart Anderson's trouser leg, the doctor looked at the wound. It was just a small hole and hadn't passed through, but was lodged in the thick muscle of the man's thigh.

'Looks like a .22,' the doc said. 'Should be easy enough to get out.' He reached into his bag and retrieved a thin pair of tweezers that looked more like pliers.

'This'll hurt a tad,' he said. 'You got any whiskey?'

Moon reached into his saddlebags and brought out a bottle. He pulled the cork out and took a mighty swig before handing it to Mackay.

'Take a couple o' mouthfuls,' the doc told Anderson, who was only too willing.

He took the bottle away from Anderson, wiped the top with a clean handkerchief and took a swig himself, before pouring some on the open wound.

Anderson gritted his teeth together as the whiskey burned into the small hole, but he made no sound.

The doc then inserted the tweezers until he felt the hardness of the bullet. Deftly, he widened the tweezers and got a good grip of the slug. Slowly, he pulled it out. All the while Anderson didn't utter a sound, but sweat was pouring down his face.

'There it is,' Mackay said, holding the bullet up for Anderson to see.

'I'll keep that, Doc,' Anderson said. 'A souvenir.'

'I ain't finished yet,' the doc said. 'Take another swig o' whiskey, maybe put this twig between your teeth and grip hard.'

Taking out a small bottle, he unscrewed the top and tipped a small amount of black powder over the wound.

'Ready?' asked Mackay.

'As I'll ever be,' Anderson said, knowing what was coming up. He gripped the twig between his teeth and closed his eyes.

Taking a Lucifer from his vest pocket, the doctor ignited the black powder. There was a small flash that lasted a mere second and soon the smell of burning flesh filled the air.

'There, that'll stop any infection.' He took a small, white pad from his bag and placed it over the wound, then a clean bandage to bind the leg.

'Try and keep off the leg for a few days. After that you should be fine.' The doctor began to pack his bag.

'How much do I owe you, Doc?' Anderson asked.

'No charge,' he replied. 'Another day or two and you'd be dead.' Then he froze. Behind him, he heard a mighty slap and a shot fired into the air. He turned to see his horse and buggy careening down the trail.

'Can't let you live, Doc,' Moon said

matter of factly.

'You can't kill me,' Mackay said. 'I got patients who might die and pregnant women to attend to. I won't say a word about this, you have my word as a doctor and humanitarian.'

★ ★ ★

Reuben reined in abruptly. Ahead, he could see the rear end of a buggy and a man holding a gun, standing to the right of the trail.

He was too far away to get a good look at the man's face, so, ground-tethering his horse, he inched forward, using the trees as cover, careful not to step on dead branches or twigs.

He got within one hundred feet of the man when he recognized him: it was Moon. The face was etched into his brain, as were the faces of all on the Wanted posters in his saddlebags.

Then a frightened horse, towing the empty buggy, flew past him. The animal's ears were pinned back, and the whites of his eyes were showing. Clearly, the slap and shot had been used to get rid of the buggy.

But why?

In a flash, Reuben worked it out. Moon had broken Anderson out of jail, and ridden on for a doctor for Anderson's leg. If he didn't act swiftly, the next shot would be aimed at the doc.

Slowly and carefully, Reuben raised his Winchester and sighted down the long barrel. The cross-wires were per. fectly aligned with Moon's chest.

Taking a deep breath, he held it and gently squeezed the trigger.

Even from this distance, his aim was true. He could even see the look of shock on Moon's face as he flew backwards and landed in the dirt.

Reuben waited a full minute, making sure the body didn't move. Satisfied that Moon was either dead or unconscious, Reuben stood, Winchester levelled at waist height, and walked towards the large oak where he'd seen Moon and the buggy.

Anderson must be there.

Reuben moved to his right, entering the small copse; at least he'd have some cover and also be to the right of the oak — hopefully unseen — and make sure it was Anderson and see if he recognized the other man.

Moving as stealthily and as silently as an Indian, Reuben reached the end of the copse. The oak tree was to his left. He saw the standing man first: small, a beer belly obvious, what little hair he had was grey, and he was holding what looked like a doctor's bag.

Reuben sussed the situation quickly. Moon had forced the doctor to tend to Anderson, then, when he had finished, spooked the buggy horse and was about to kill him.

Moon couldn't leave a witness.

He shifted his gaze — and his Winchester — to the left and saw a naked leg stretched out on the ground.

Anderson!

He looked back at the doc and decided to make his presence felt. Standing, he waved, then placed a finger to his lips.

The old man got the message.

'Henry?' a strangled voice called out. 'Hey, Henry, you OK?' Anderson hoped and prayed that his partner was playing possum.

He wasn't.

Henry Moon was dead, there was no doubt about it.

* * *

A mile and a half further back down the trail, Clarke suddenly reined in and cocked his head to one side.

'You hear that?' he asked Adams.

'Hear what?'

'I thought I heard a gunshot up ahead,' Adams replied.

'You're imaginin' it,' Clarke said.

'That weren't no imagination,' Adams said angrily.

Then they both heard the thundering sound of an approaching horse.

The two men immediately moved to the side of the trail, under a cottonwood —

and waited, rifles drawn and cocked.

From around a bend in the trail, a foam-flecked horse appeared towing what seemed to be an empty buggy.

'What the hell?' Clarke said.

'Reckon that shot spooked it. But why and who?' Adams said.

'Only one way to find out,' Clarke replied.

'Keep your rifle handy,' Adams said, and edged his horse forward at a walking pace.

* * *

Reuben raised his Winchester and, taking careful aim, loosed a shot that brought a scream from the man with the bare leg.

The doc fell to his knees, fear etched on his podgy face.

Slowly, Reuben approached the oak, making sure the wounded man wasn't armed. But he saw that both the man's hands were gripping his leg.

'Well, well,' Reuben said. 'Seems you didn't get far, Anderson.'

'You son of a bitch,' was all Anderson said.

'You better take a look at him, Doc, before we take him in.'

'Take him in where?' the doctor asked.

'Where'd you come from?' asked Reuben.

'Cannon Falls, it's around an hour away, at least,' Mackay replied.

'Then that's where we're heading,' Reuben said.

'I better take a look at his leg — again,' the doc said. 'He might bleed to death.'

'OK, but make it quick.'

'What's he done?' the medico asked as he kneeled beside Anderson, opening his medicine bag once more.

'He was with the James-Younger gang that tried to rob the bank — and failed miserably,' Reuben said.

The doc removed the slug from Anderson's leg. There was no finesse this time, and Anderson moaned and cried at the pain.

In no time at all, he had bound the wound and looked towards Reuben.

'Bring one of the horses over,' Reuben

told the doctor, who obeyed immediately.

'I'll need a hand to lift him across the saddle,' Reuben said, as he whistled for his horse. It appeared within a few minutes. Reuben grabbed a coil of rope and hung it on his shoulder.

'Take his feet, Doc. We'll lay him belly down across the saddle.' Reuben grabbed Anderson under his armpits and lifted the heavy man. They managed to lift and carry him to the waiting horse.

Adrenalin pumping through his body, Reuben managed to raise Anderson across the horse then, uncoil.ing the rope, tied the man's feet together, then walked round the front of the horse and tied Anderson's hands with the other end of the rope, making sure it was tight.

Anderson groaned.

Grabbing the reins of the horse, he led it to his own horse.

'You OK, Doc?'

'Yeah, sure. I'll need a lift to mount up though; it's been a while since I rode a horse.'

Reuben ground-hitched both horses

and, cupping his hands for Mackay to step into, he heaved him onto the animal making sure his boots were in the stirrups.

Mounting his own horse, Reuben grabbed the reins of the third animal and they set off at a walking pace. Reuben didn't want the doctor to fall off!

* * *

Meanwhile, the Pinkerton agents were closing in on the township of Madelia, where they knew that most of the James-Younger gang were holed up.

Two of their members were killed in a shoot-out that also killed John Younger and later on, they lost another agent posing as an itinerant fieldworker at Frank James' farm, who made the mistake of asking too many questions, and it was assumed that Frank or Jesse James had shot him in cold blood.

The rest of the Younger brothers, Cole, Jim and Bob were being held in Northfield, awaiting trial, the outcome of which was beyond doubt.

Reuben and the doctor were making slow progress to Cannon Falls. It had been a long day and Reuben reckoned they only had around an hour before the sun disappeared.

He looked at the doc, who was slumped forwards in the saddle, and knew the old man was tiring fast. At this rate they wouldn't make Cannon Falls before sunset.

'Doc,' Reuben called out, 'I think we'd better find somewhere to make camp. You know this area, any sug.gestions?'

The doc reined in and thought for a while. Then he smiled.

'There's a gully about a quarter of a mile to the right. It's well hidden and surrounded by cottonwoods.'

'Sounds ideal,' Reuben said. 'Here's what we do. We leave the trail to the left and ride around fifty yards, then we follow the line of the trail for a hundred yards or so, then head right. That way, anyone following will lose track of us.'

151

The doc looked bewildered. 'Who's likely to follow us?'

'Better safe than sorry,' Reuben said. 'No way am I going to let Anderson get rescued again. The man hangs for sure.'

16

William Clarke and Alexander Adams reached the point in the path where the giant oak tree stood to their right.

Adams looked for sign.

'Buggy came as far as here and stopped a while. You can see the wheel ruts where it was parked just off the trail.'

'Look yonder,' Clarke said. 'There's a body.'

Both men walked their animals towards the prone figure.

'Well, I'll be damned!' Clarke looked at Adams. 'If that ain't Henry Moon.'

'He the one who busted Bloody Bill Anderson outa jail?' Clarke asked.

'Sure is,' Adams answered. 'So what the hell happened here?'

Both men dismounted and leant over the body.

'He dead?' Clarke asked.

'As a dodo,' Adams replied.

'A what?'

'Never mind. He's dead,' Adams said.

'The buggy pulled off the trail here,' Clarke pointed, 'coming from Cannon Falls, but then bolted the other away.'

Adams walked to the end of the buggy tracks which led to an oak tree.

He knelt and pointed at the ground. 'There's blood here, a whole heap of it and some used bandages.'

'Anderson?' Clarke said. 'Moon must have brought a doc out here to fix Anderson's leg.

'Then who shot Moon?' Adams said.

Clarke studied the ground, looking for sign.

'There's three horse prints here. One must be Anderson's, another Moon's which the doc must be riding now. So, who's the third one belong to?'

'Only one way to find out,' Adams said, 'let's follow the trail.'

★ ★ ★

Reuben led the way off the trail until they reached a rocky outcrop where he halted and dismounted.

Breaking off a cottonwood branch, he walked back to the trail and carefully levelled out their hoofprints and, walking backwards, brushed his own tracks. Anyone fol.lowing would come to a dead halt.

Mounting up, they rode for around two hundred yards before returning to cross the trail. Again, Reuben dis. mounted and smoothed out their hoofprints before leading on towards the gully.

'That was a mighty neat trick,' the doc remarked.

'Been on the trail a long time, Doc,' Reuben said matter of factly.

'The gully is about half a mile,' Mackay added. 'Can't say I won't be relieved to get out o' this saddle.'

'You lead on, Doc, we'll follow.'

Anderson hadn't uttered a word since they'd tied him to the horse. Either he was dead or just plain asleep. Either way,

155

Reuben decided to gag him.

'Hold on there, Doc, just gonna make sure Anderson can't make any noise and give away our position.'

'You ain't gonna shoot him, are you?' the doctor asked.

Reuben grinned. 'That's tempting, Doc, but no, just gonna gag him.'

Reuben dismounted and untied his bandanna. As he fixed it around Anderson's mouth, the man grunted. *So he was still alive*, thought Reuben.

Mounting up, the doctor led on towards the gully.

17

'Looks like the third rider came up the trail, headin' towards Cannon Falls. The buggy and one rider were comin' from Cannon Falls.' Clarke paused.

'Well, whoever killed Moon wasn't a member of the gang. You reckon he was tracking them?' Adams said.

'Looks that way,' Clarke said.

'It'll be dark soon, we'd better make camp here and set off at first light. What d'you think?' Adams said, looking towards the west and the slowly-sinking sun.

'Sounds good to me,' Clarke said. 'We'll ground-hitch the horses; there's plenty of grass to the side of the trail.'

Both men dismounted and removed their saddles and saddlebags and led the animals to a patch of lush grass just behind the oak tree.

'Plenty of kindlin' here, too,' said Clarke. 'I'll water the horses and you get a fire goin', I sure am hungry.'

Pretty soon the fire was burning and coffee was brewing. Adams pulled out some beans and bacon and a heap of nearly-stale bread.

Twenty minutes later, both men lit a quirly and settled down, using their saddles as pillows.

It was full dark now and the sky was pitch black. No clouds to obscure the view of the millions of stars.

They threw their butts into the fire, added more wood and settled in to sleep.

⋆ ⋆ ⋆

Reuben and Mackay finally reached the gully. It was an ideal camp site. A dried-up river bed, tall rocks on either side, worn down from when the river was in full flow, and trees behind them.

Unlike Adams and Clarke, there would be no fire for Reuben and the doc.

'I only got some jerky,' Reuben said.

'I have some freshly-baked sourdough bread and a bottle o' whiskey — for

158

medicinal purposes o' course.' A smile spread across his lined face.

'Sounds like a feast to me,' Reuben said, and grinned at the doctor.

They took care of the horses first; Reuben gave all three animals some barley and oats and filled his Stetson with water. The grass on the river bed was sparse, but they'd only be here till dawn.

Reuben took the saddle off his horse, then the doc's.

'What about him?' the doctor asked.

'He stays where he is,' Reuben said as he tied up the horse Anderson was spread on, making sure there was grass beneath its feet.

Then, reaching into his saddlebag he brought out some strips of jerky, while the doc retrieved the bread and bottle of whiskey.

Pulling out the cork, the doc said, 'Your good health,' and raised the bottle to his lips and took a mighty swig before handing the bottle to Reuben.

Not being a heavy drinker, Reuben took a mouthful and coughed as the fiery liquid went down his throat, then both men tucked into their jerky and bread. The doctor was sipping whiskey in between mouthfuls of bread; Reuben declined when offered.

Their meagre meal over, Reuben grabbed his canteen and drank his fill before passing it to Mackay.

Taking another mouthful of whiskey, the doctor re-corked the bottle and declined the offer of water.

'I got a tarp and a bedroll,' Reuben said. 'I'll check Anderson's and see if he has the same.'

'You're in luck, Doc, there's a tarp and bedroll here so at least you'll keep warmish.'

The sun had finally sunk below the horizon and the temperature was dropping dramatically.

'It's gonna be a cold one tonight,' Reuben said.

No sooner had he said that than a huge clap of thunder roared, seeming to shake the ground.

'Jesus,' the doc said. 'Damn near gave

me a heart attack.'

A minute later, a slight drizzle started to fall.

Both men grabbed their tarps and covered themselves as best they could. It was bad enough being cold without being soaking wet as well.

Reuben looked to the west and saw the range of moun.tains to the west. 'It might be a drizzle here,' he said, 'but it'll be torrential up in the mountains. We can't stay here.'

'Why ever not?' the doctor asked. 'We got cover, and we're well hidden from anyone findin' us.'

'You ever seen a flash flood?' Reuben asked.

'Not first hand, but I've heard o' them,' the doc replied.

'We're in a gully. It used to be a river or is the outcome of previous flash floods. We gotta get out of here to higher ground. And we need to do it *now*!'

18

The clap of distant thunder woke both Clarke and Adams from a deep sleep. For a moment, they thought they were being shot at: then the lightning came.

Both men were temporarily blinded as the sheet lightning cast an eerie blue-white light across the landscape.

'Should we head for Cannon Falls?' asked Adams.

'No. Too risky, when the rain's so heavy, you can't see more'n five feet and that lightnin' is deadly. We need to tether the horses, so they don't bolt, and then settle by the oak under our tarps and wait it out.'

Adams secured their mounts and removed the saddles just before the rain started.

It began gently, a mere drizzle but, as the dark clouds neared them, forked lightning filled the sky and within three seconds thunder rapped out and the drizzle became a downpour of such ferocity that Adams felt as if someone was pouring buckets of water over his head.

He made it to the oak tree and pulled the tarp over his head and shoulders, but already he was soaked through and freezing cold.

It was going to be a long, long night.

* * *

Reuben, towing Anderson's horse, followed by Mackay, eased their mounts along the gully floor.

Rocks littered the trail, evidence of previous flash floods and the last thing they needed was for one of the horses to go lame.

After another thirty minutes, the rocks on either side began to get smaller until, one hundred yards ahead, they saw a break in the gully. Green grass came into view and their animals snorted in anticipation.

Riding up the grassy slope was no easy

163

matter. The ground was soaked, and the horses had great difficulty in keeping their hoofs from sliding backwards. Eventually, they reached the top and there was an audible sigh from the doc as both men dismounted.

'I ain't never been on a horse for so long in my life!' the doctor wheezed.

'Well, we'll hold up here awhiles, see what happens next,' Reuben said.

No sooner had he finished speaking when they heard a distant rumble.

'That sure weren't no thunder,' the doc said, staring down at the gully.

The thundering rumble grew louder, and the two men just stared as a trickle of water began to run down the gully, getting stronger and stronger until it was a torrent carrying rocks, timber and anything in its path.

'Jeez!' was all Reuben was able to say.

The water level began to rise as more and more debris joined in the rush of water. The noise was deafening as debris pounded the side walls of the gully.

'We got out of there just in time,'

Mackay said. 'We wouldn't have stood a chance down there.'

'Water!' Anderson's voice broke through the sound of the roaring water.

Reuben fetched his canteen and, lifting Anderson's head by his hair, poured water down his throat.

'Food,' Anderson said.

Reuben shoved a strip of jerky in his mouth and watched as the man chewed hungrily.

The rain stopped as suddenly as it had begun.

'Well, at least we can dry out some,' Reuben said.

At that point the moon made a rare appearance and in the eerie blue light, Reuben looked around the landscape. He saw no movement. And the light didn't last long. But he did see the muzzle flash!

'Down, now!' he shouted at the doc.

The doctor was no fool and asked no questions as he flung himself onto the wet grass.

'Hold your fire, mister,' Reuben

shouted. 'We got a prisoner here from the Northfield Bank robbery.'

'I'm a Pinkerton Agent searching for a man called Anderson,' the man replied.

'So you shoot first and talk after,' Reuben said laconically.

'Can't be too careful out here,' the man replied.

'Well, we got Anderson and I'm taking him in to Cannon Falls to stand trial as soon as the circuit judge arrives,' stated Reuben.

Turning around Reuben whispered, 'Sorry, Doc, I don't even know your name.'

'It's Mackay, Duncan Mackay.'

'I'm Reuben Chisholm.'

'Good to meet you, Mr Chisholm,' the doc grinned.

'You, too, Doc Mackay.'

'Duncan.'

'Reuben.'

It seemed ridiculous, but they shook hands.

As Reuben turned around, he saw the lone horseman, Winchester across his lap, walking his horse towards them. 'Mind if I join you folks?' he asked. 'Not with that rifle out of its scabbard,' Reuben replied. Slowly, the man raised the Winchester and slid it into its sheath. 'No problem,' the man said, halting his horse. 'You got any papers on you?' Reuben asked. 'In my saddlebags. OK if I dismount?' the man said. Reuben already had his Colt in his right hand, hidden from the man's view.

Slowly, the man dismounted and carefully pulled up the flap of one of his saddlebags, bringing out a sheaf of papers. He let the flap drop down and approached Reuben.

'That's close enough, mister,' Reuben said. 'Just put

them papers on the ground and step back aways.' The man did as he was told and reversed several paces. Keeping his gun levelled at the man, Reuben stepped forward and picked up the papers. 'What's your name, mister?' Reuben asked. 'Ely Watson,' came the reply. Reuben showed the letter of confirmation to Doc

Mackay. 'Seems real enough to me,' the doctor said. Reuben took the papers back and holstered his Colt. 'OK, Mr Watson — ' 'Call me Ely.' 'OK, Ely. Why are you trailing us?' Reuben asked. 'I wasn't,' Ely replied. 'I was tracking Anderson after he was broken out of jail.'

'But you followed us,' Reuben said.

'I had a buggy careen past me on the trail and followed the tracks. I came upon the body of Henry Moon, figured some of the James-Younger gang had had an argument and Moon lost out. I searched the area, found hoof prints. Then I saw the blood at the base of an old oak tree and the buggy trail led on to Cannon Falls. So I followed them. Then the storm came, and every sign was washed away, but I figured that's where what was left of the James-Younger gang were headed.'

'What was left?' Reuben queried.

'Most of the gang were either killed or wounded, including the Youngers,' Ely replied. 'Frank was wounded but he and his brother, Jesse, managed to escape Northfield.'

'You reckon Frank and Jesse are in Cannon Falls?' Reuben asked.

'Nope. Last I heard they'd headed for the Dakotas.'

'So how come you trailed us?' Reuben asked.

'Pure luck. I saw three horses and figured it was part of the gang,' Watson said. 'That's how come I fired first, trying to cut the odds down some.'

'Sounds reasonable to me,' the doc said.

'OK. We leave at first light. No point risking the horses in the darkness,' Reuben said.

'I'd better take a look at Anderson's leg. We can't keep him trussed up like that all night, he'll die,' the doc said and spread his tarp on the grass. Reuben and Ely followed shortly and, pretty soon, all slept.

* * *

Clarke and Adams had a much better night than Reuben, Duncan, Anderson and Ely. They'd found some relatively dry kindling in the lee of the oak tree and managed to light a fire.

Coffee was soon boiling, and Adams added some fat.back bacon and beans to a skillet. Steam was rising from Adam's clothes as the fire slowly dried him out.

Out of the blue, the crack of a rifle shot rang out. The shooter missed both men but hit their fire. Instinctively, Adams and Clarke rolled left and right, bringing their side-irons into play.

The stranger's horse rose on its rear legs as shots were exchanged, but Adams and Clarke could not see their attacker. All they could make out was the muzzle flash of the stranger's weapon, but that kept moving around, never staying in the same place for more than a second or two.

The storm had long passed, and the clouds began to get lighter and eventually, the moon cast its eerie light across the landscape.

It was just what William Clarke had prayed for. The stranger, firing from a nervous mount, had little chance of hitting them, but Clarke took careful aim with his Winchester and loosed a single shot.

His slug creased the horse's head and hit the rider in the chest, knocking him backwards, landing hard on the ground some six feet behind his now madly galloping mount.

The man didn't move.

'Wonder who the hell he is — was?' Adams said.

'Only one way to find out,' Clarke replied.

Slowly and carefully, both men crawled forwards, in case the man was playing possum.

'Jeez!' Clarke gasped.

'What? You never seen a stiff afore,' Adams laughed.

'He's wearin' a tin star,' Clarke replied.

'Damnation!' Adams had stopped laughing.

Clarke was silent for a moment, trying

to work out a plan, then: 'You drag the body into the bush, and make sure it can't be seen from the trail. I'll unsaddle the horse and set it off away from town. OK?' He pulled off the sheriff's tin star and put it in his vest pocket. 'Souvenir,' he said. 'Might come in handy one day.' He grinned.

★ ★ ★

Reuben sat bolt upright, his Colt already in his hand.

Although the shots he'd heard were fairly distant, they were still too close for comfort.

But his attention was drawn to something else.

Ten feet from the dying fire he saw a pair of bright eyes. Too small for a grizzly, but any wild animal could be dangerous.

He quickly grabbed some more kindling and built the fire up, the light spreading, and he was able to see what the unblinking, bright eyes belonged to.

It was a cougar, and looked ready to

make an attack.

The animal took two steps forward, its eyes remaining level.

It was now within leaping range and Reuben knew he had seconds to get off a killing shot.

Like a bullet, the animal leapt through the air, its claws extended, ready to maul.

Holding the Colt in both hands, he loosed off a shot.

His aim was true. The slug took the animal between the eyes, but its momentum carried the now-dead body forwards and the cougar landed on Reuben, its claws gashing both his arms as he tried to protect his head.

The weight of the animal was making it difficult to breathe, and he had to heave his chest to breathe in and out.

Then he felt the pain in both arms.

Doc Mackay raised himself on one elbow and didn't believe what his eyes were telling him.

As quickly as his old body would allow, he got his bag and went across to Reuben. He exhaled a breath of relief as he saw Reuben's eyes move and look at him.

'Help shift this lump off me, Doc. I can hardly breathe.'

With Ely's help, they managed to shift the heavy, limp body of the cougar from Reuben's chest, and immediately, Reuben rolled out, taking deep breaths.

'Let me take a look at your arms, blood is soakin' through your shirt.'

Taking some scissors from his bag, Doc Mackay cut both sleeves off and took a long, hard look at the lacerations.

'Some o' these will need stitchin',' the doc said. 'You got any whiskey?'

''Fraid not, Doc.'

'Good job I always carry some,' a grin spread across his face as he reached into his bag again.

Pulling out the cork with his teeth, the doc took a mighty swig, smacked his lips together and said: 'That's better.'

'Might be better for you,' Reuben said through gritted teeth.

'Take a couple o' slugs, Reuben. This is gonna hurt a tad. I'll bandage up the smaller lacerations, but there's two or three that'll need some stitchin'. OK?'

'You're the doc,' Reuben replied, raising the bottle to his lips and taking in two large gulps.

'Ready?' the doc asked.

'Ready as I'll ever be,' Reuben said, and clamped his teeth together as the doctor dabbed whiskey on the small cuts.

It took a further half hour to apply the bandages, and the pain began to ease up some.

'Now for the tricky part,' the doc said. 'Take some more whiskey.'

Reuben didn't need to be asked twice.

'Now swallow some of this,' Mackay said.

'What is it?' Reuben asked.

'It's laudanum, it'll help with the pain.'

The doc carefully threaded a needle and began sewing.

To take his mind off the pain, Reuben asked: 'So you didn't hear two gunshots?'

'Nope. First thing I heard was your pistol,' the doc replied.

'They were a way off, back down the

trail, but I figure someone's following us,' Reuben said.

'Well, there's not much we can do about that 'til day.light. You rest up and I'll keep a lookout,' the doc said and Reuben closed his eyes, both arms throbbing. Luckily, it was his left arm that was worst, and he felt he could still use his right hand to shoot his pistol.

With that thought in mind, he slept.

19

Adams was nearly at the edge of the brush and tangle-weed when he heard a shot.

Both men froze. They knew it was a long way off, but had no idea whether it was behind them or in front of them.

'You get a fix on that shot?' Adams asked.

'Nope. You?'

'Too much echo. Let's get this done.'

The two men managed to dump the body of the sheriff, then remove the saddle — and weapons — from the sheriff's horse and, slapping its rump hard, sent it running away from town.

'We'll have to wait for daybreak before we move on, it's too dark to risk losin' a mount,' Clarke said.

★ ★ ★

The rest of the night passed peacefully enough.

It was quiet and, for Doc Mackay, too quiet.

Then, as he cast his eyes to the east, he saw the satisfy.ing glow of deep red as the sun slowly rose, sending shafts of bright light across the land. In a matter of moments, the darkness was eaten up as the sun rose higher and higher, casting deep shadows from rocky outcrops.

He added some more kindling to the dying embers of the fire, filled the coffee pot with some Arbuckle's, and shook Reuben's boot to wake him up.

In an instant, Reuben sat bolt upright, his Colt already drawn.

'Well, you sure don't change much,' the doc commented. 'Even with a damaged arm.'

'The right arm feels fine, Doc. The left one's a bit sore and stiff, but that'll pass soon enough.'

'Good. Coffee's on, then we better break camp and head for town.'

'Sooner I hand Anderson over to the

sheriff, the better,' Reuben said.

'I better wake Anderson and give him a coffee before we set off,' Doc Mackay said.

Reuben looked around and saw the cougar for the first time.

'Man, that's a big critter.' Reuben stood looking down at the dead animal, every part of its body bulging with muscle. 'I sure was lucky I got a shot off,' he added.

'Closest I've ever been to a cougar,' Ely said.

The doc grunted as he kicked one of Anderson's boots to wake him up, then handed him a tin mug of coffee.

'Leg's killing me, Doc,' Anderson said.

'We'll be in Cannon Falls in one to two hours at this rate. I'll fix it up then — when you're in jail!'

Anderson took a sip of the coffee and then looked the doc in the eye. 'I won't be in jail fer long,' and smirked.

'Long enough for the scaffold to be built,' the medico replied and walked back to Reuben by the fire.

'We better drink up and get going,' Reuben said. 'How long till we hit town?'

'No more'n one or two hours, if we keep this slow pace up,' the doc replied. 'Funny, Anderson asked the same question.'

'I gotta feeling Anderson's hoping to catch up with the gang who tried to raid the Northfield bank,' Reuben said.

'Well, if'n he is, he's in for a huge disappointment,' the doc laughed.

'How so?'

'Word has it that Frank and Jesse headed for the Dakotas and what was left o' the gang split up and headed towards Madelia. The Pinkerton Agents are already there. What the gang don't know is that there ain't a town within a hundred mile radius o' Northfield that ain't on the lookout for them.'

'We better break camp and head for Cannon Falls. You help Ely pack up here and I'll sort Anderson out. Then we ride.'

* * *

180

At almost exactly the same time, Clarke and Adams broke camp. Pouring the dregs of the coffee pot over the fire and kicking sand over it, they made sure the fire was out before saddling up and riding on towards Cannon Falls.

They'd ridden around two miles when Clarke suddenly called a halt.

'What's up, pard?' Adams asked.

'Look at the trail. You can just about make out the wheel ruts of the buggy, but look. There are four sets of hoof prints there. *Four*!'

'Maybe the sheriff's horse was returning to Cannon Falls,' Adams said.

'Unlikely. The ground is soft after the rain. Them hoof prints are deep — meanin' there was a rider on all four horses.

'Well, it sure as hell wasn't Henry Moon, that's fer sure.'

Adams grinned.

'Or the sheriff,' Clarke added.

'So who the hell was it? A member of the gang? He didn't come along the trail, he joined it here,' Adams observed.

'They're still headin' for Cannon Falls, so I guess we'll find out there,' Clarke said. 'I just hope it's the guys we're lookin' for.'

* * *

Doc Mackay was riding beside Reuben, while Ely had the reins of Anderson's horse secured round his pommel.

'You're quiet, Doc. Anything on your mind?' Reuben asked.

'Well, since you asked, I been wonderin' why you were so keen on bringin' Anderson in.'

'You mean apart from his being a murdering, raping, scumbag?' Reuben answered.

'Good enough reason,' the doc agreed.

'He rode with Quantrill, and the two fellas who killed my wife were also ex-Quantrill. It's them I'm after. Anderson is just the bait.'

Reuben reached inside his vest pocket and pulled out two Wanted posters.

'William Clarke and Alexander

Adams.' Reuben handed the posters to the doc.

'Well, can't say I recognize them. Mind you, I've never been more than ten miles out o' Cannon Falls.' He handed back the posters.

'I'm hoping that using Anderson, instead of me trying to find Clarke and Adams, they'll find me.'

'And then what?' the doc asked.

'I'm gonna kill them,' Reuben stated flatly.

20

After a thirty-minute ride in silence, Doc Mackay suddenly pointed ahead and said, 'There she is. Cannon Falls.'

Reuben could vaguely make out some buildings and breathed a sigh of relief.

'Should be there in less than thirty minutes,' the doc added gleefully.

'Can't be soon enough for me,' Reuben said.

'You ain't keeping me in jail for long,' Anderson croaked.

'You ain't wrong there,' Ely said. 'The Circuit Judge and jury will see to that.'

Anderson laughed. 'You think that's gonna happen? I'll be free within two days.'

'Dream on, Anderson,' Ely said. 'You ain't got no Henry Moon to help you this time.'

'I got others,' Anderson said.

'Yeah, right,' Reuben replied.

The doc and Reuben looked at each

other and grinned. From what Ely had told them, there was no gang left and they were sure that both Frank and Jesse James wouldn't risk returning to rescue a scumbag like Anderson.

'You're gonna hang, Anderson. There's no two ways about that.' Reuben didn't even look back at him, a man he detested.

★ ★ ★

They arrived on the outskirts of Cannon Falls, and like most small towns, there were little shacks, most of which were run down. Reuben wondered how they still stood.

There were one or two people about, shabby, hungover probably.

As they progressed, so the shacks became small houses, some with picket fences and a small plot of land mostly growing vegetables, but there were a few flower plots, too, adding some colour to the sun-bleached clapboards of the buildings.

Stores began to appear: a milliner's, gun shop, general store and a barber's. The sheriff's office was at the end of the shops, set back slightly, on the corner of what passed for Main Street and a broad alley lined with small houses, all neatly painted.

Opposite the sheriff's office was the doctor's surgery, a saloon and next to that a casino, both of which were open, but scarcely populated. Reuben checked his Hunter; it was 9.30a.m., maybe too early for most folk.

Reuben dismounted and knocked on the sheriff's door.

There was no reply.

He tried the door-knob, but it was locked.

'Ain't no sheriff today, fella,' a passer-by said.

'How come?' Reuben asked.

'Cos it's Tuesday,' the man replied as if that explained everything.

'So?' Reuben looked puzzled.

'Tuesday's fishin' day, he won't be back 'til Thursday, unless the fish are

186

bitin', then it could be Friday. Mind you, if they ain't bitin', he might be back today, got no patience that man.'

'Is there a deputy?' Reuben asked.

'Nope. Never had the need for one.'

'You ever hear about Bloody Bill Anderson?' Reuben asked.

'Sure have, 'sposed to be the meanest critter around,' the man replied.

'Well, that's him,' Reuben pointed at his prisoner.

'Son of a gun,' the townsman said, his mouth agape. 'Hey!' the man shouted, 'Look who we — '

'Keep your voice down and don't let anyone know who we got here; there ain't gonna be no lynching here. When's the circuit judge due?' Reuben asked.

'Hell, you better ask the mayor that one. I jus' run the General Store.'

'OK. So where do I find the mayor?' Reuben asked, his patience wearing thin.

'Oh. He'll be with the sheriff,' the man replied nonchalantly.

Reuben drew his Colt and pointed it at the man's head.

'Mister, I'm gonna ask you one more question,' Reuben said, his eyes as cold as the metal of his gun.

The man visibly shrank and began to shake.

'Who's in charge of this shit-hole?'

'W-w-well. I guess I am,' the man stammered.

Reuben was almost at the end of his tether. He felt like

shooting the man just for the hell of it. Another townsman approached the men. 'Don't take no notice of ol' Jake here. He ain't quite right in the head. ou need help here, Doc, sir?' 'I need to get my prisoner locked up and wait for the circuit judge,' Reuben said.

'An' who is this prisoner?' the man asked. 'My name is Chuck, by the way.'

'It's Bloody Bill Anderson,' Jake said with a big grin on his face.

Reuben just stared at the man.

'I'll get the keys to the sheriff's office an' we'll get him in a cell, pronto.'

'Thanks, Chuck,' Reuben said.

'Good to see you back, Doc,' Chuck

grinned.

'Believe me, Chuck, it's good to be back.'

'I'll get the keys, it won't take a moment,' Chuck said, 'an' then we can get a drink and some grub.'

'Sounds good to me,' Mackay smiled.

'OK, Jake. On your way,' Reuben said to the man, less harshly this time, now that he knew the man was a bit 'simple'.

Chuck returned with a bunch of keys and started trying to unlock the sheriff's office. At the fifth attempt, he found the right key and opened the door.

It was dark in the office, the shutters were drawn and there was a musty smell.

'I take it the sheriff doesn't spend much time in here,' Reuben remarked as the undid the shutters.

'We get the occasional drunk, but little else,' Chuck responded. 'I'll get the stove lit an' coffee on. Here's the keys to the cells, let's get that critter locked up.'

'I'll see to his leg and get that sewn up, then let us get some decent grub.' The doc and Ely went outside and helped

Anderson off his horse.

Anderson laughed out loud as they walked him through the sheriff's office and into the cell block.

'You think you can keep me in here?' he laughed again. 'I'll be out afore nightfall,' he bragged.

'See that cot, Anderson? You'll be handcuffed to it, and the cot is anchored in concrete. Still think you'll escape?' Reuben said smugly.

Anderson didn't utter another word as he was placed on the hard cot. Then his wrists were handcuffed to metal bars on either side of it.

Reuben went back to the front office and gave Ely a hand getting the stove lit and the coffee brewing. They both winced as the yells came from the cells as Doc Mackay went to work on Anderson's leg.

No whiskey or laudanum this time.

The doc came through to the front office and his mouth watered as he smelled the aroma of the Arbuckle's that filled the room.

'I guess we'll have to take shifts in keeping an eye on Anderson. I wouldn't put anything past him,' Reuben said. 'I'll take first watch. Chuck, are you with us?'

'Sure thing,' Chuck replied.

'Could you sort out some grub for us?' Ely asked.

'Yeah, I'll go over to Sally's Eatery; she's a damn fine cook.'

Chuck downed his coffee and left the sheriff's office.

'Well, seems to me I'm not needed any more, so I'll mosey on home, get cleaned up and see what messages I've missed.'

'Thanks for all your help, Doc,' Reuben said.

'Yeah, thanks Doc, see you in the morning.'

21

'Hold up,' Adams said.

'What's up now?' Clarke asked.

'They left the trail here,' Adams pointed to the tracks.

'Maybe it's a short cut. How far's Cannon Falls from here?' Clarke asked.

'How the hell would I know? I ain't ever heard of it afore and certainly never bin there,' Adams said.

'We better keep our eyes peeled,' Clarke said. 'It gets rocky up yonder, so the trail will be hard to follow.'

'OK, lead on.'

The two men rode in silence, glancing at the ground and then left and right, making sure they weren't about to ride into an ambush.

They reached a flat, rock plateau which gave them a better view of what lay ahead.

'There's grassland down there,' Clarke said. 'We'll soon pick up their trail.'

'You know what?' Adams said. 'I reckon they camped down yonder, that's why they left the trail.'

'We'll soon find out,' Clarke said, and led his horse gin.gerly down the slope until they hit the flatter grassland, where the animals stopped of their own accord and started to munch on the rich, green grass.

Moving on, they'd covered only fifty yards when Clarke reined in and raised his Stetson.

'Holy shit!' he exclaimed. 'Look at that!'

'Sure is one big cat,' Adams said, and dismounted, drawing his Colt.

He approached the cougar cautiously, not sure if the animal was dead or alive.

He hoped the former.

Tapping the animal with his foot, nothing happened. He kicked harder, but the animal didn't move.

'It's dead. But there's blood here on the ground and on the animal's claws. He sure did someone some damage.'

'Who'd you think it was?' asked Clarke.

'You ask some damn fool questions! How the hell would I know?'

'That pelt would fetch a few dollars,' Clarke said.

'Oh, so you know how to skin a cat?' Adams said deri.sively.

'Well, not exactly, but it can't be that difficult,' Clarke said defensively.

'Yeah, sure.' Adams snorted.

'OK, OK, it was just an idea.' Clarke looked peeved.

'Let's get moving. The tracks lead this way.' He pointed north-west. 'There's still four riders, and one of them knows this terrain well,' Adams said.

Taking a final look at the cougar, Clarke reluctantly dug his heels into his mount and followed Adams.

Within fifteen minutes, they emerged back onto the trail to Cannon Falls.

'Can't be much further now,' Clarke said.

'Can't be that close, otherwise they wouldn't have bedded down for the night,' Adams said.

'There's their tracks, still four of 'em.'

Clarke pointed out. 'They don't seem to be in much of a hurry.'

Suddenly a shot broke the peaceful silence. It wasn't that far away. Then another. Both shots told Clarke and Adams they were rifles, probably Sharps.

22

Adams took out his army issue telescope and scanned the area ahead. 'There's two fellas about two hundred yards down the trail. There's no tracks here, so they must have come from town,' Adams said.

'Can you see what they were shootin' at?' Clarke asked.

'Well, it sure as hell wasn't us. As I guessed, they're both holding Sharps,' Adams replied, and he peered at the area where the two riders were looking.

'Well, I'll be,' Adams said. 'If it ain't a small herd of buffalo! Must be a half mile away at least, and they got one.'

'They headin' for it yet?' Clarke asked.

'They sure are,' Adams replied. 'Let's get going, they ain't interested in us.'

Adams and Clarke walked their animals slowly and silently along the trail, not wanting to attract any attention.

But the stampeding herd forced them to change tactics, for they had veered west, heading towards the trail — and them!

Immediately, the two buffalo hunters turned and chased the terrified animals, their Sharps firing as they galloped full pelt after their prey.

'Let's turn back a-ways, with any luck the herd will pass us by. I just hope those two fellas don't start shooting at us!' They both reined their horses around and galloped back the way they had come.

The herd was closing in on them, thick dust filled the air as the heavy animals' hoofs pounded the arid ground.

The noise made was like thunder. Although there were only twenty or thirty animals, they made the ground tremble as they galloped towards the track.

Then it seemed that luck was on their side. The herd changed track once more, heading north at a furious pace, still followed by the hunters.

Clarke and Adams reined in and watched the chase. The dust was choking, but lessened as the herd got further away.

197

Breathing in the dust made both men cough and spit into the sand before pulling up their bandannas. They took deep breaths, mainly of relief.

'That was too close for comfort,' Clarke said and, lowering his bandanna, took a long drink from his canteen. Adams reached into his saddlebag and took out a bottle of bourbon. Taking out the cork with his teeth and holding it in his left hand, he lifted the bottle to his lips, taking three or four deep gulps before passing it to Clarke who, still coughing, shook his head.

Adams replaced the cork and put the bottle back in his saddlebag.

'Well, let's get moving. I can't even see or hear them damn buffalo, so they'll be well gone, but we need to keep our eyes open. OK?'

* * *

The sun was at its highest, and the heat was building up as the two men rode towards Cannon Falls. Their animals were coated in a sheen of sweat — as were both men. Mirages ahead showed lakes of cool, clear water, only to disappear the nearer they got and then reappear further ahead. The more water they thought they'd seen, the thirstier they became.

'Damn, I hope this town ain't much further. How much water you got?' Clarke asked.

''Bout half a canteen, as well as half a bottle of bourbon,' Adams said.

'I got about the same. But I'm resistin' takin' a drink as long as I can,' Clarke said.

They slowed their galloping animals down to a trot; the last thing they needed was for them to die of exhaustion.

'Don't worry,' Adams sounded confident. 'I'm sure Cannon Falls is no more than half an hour away. We'll be OK.'

'Yeah, but we can't just ride in in broad daylight. We've no idea who might already be there,' Clarke replied.

Suddenly their mounts' ears pricked up and they neighed softly.

'I gotta feeling they smell something,' Adams said. They rounded a sharp bend in the trail, passing huge rocks and there, to their right, was a stream.

Adams patted his horse's neck. 'Good boy. Good boy.'

Without being led, the animals headed straight for the small stream, which was obviously, during the winter months, a raging torrent of water, turning this small stream into a dangerous river.

Both men dismounted, emptied their canteens and refilled them with the cool water and hung them back on the pommels of their saddles. Cupping their hands, they scooped water into their parched mouths, splashing the water over their heads. The feeling was one of relief as well as refreshing.

Clarke removed his boots and sank his feet into the water, then filled his Stetson with water and poured it over his head.

'Boy, that sure feels good.' He grinned.

'You look like a drowned rat,' Adams smirked. Nevertheless, he followed suit and breathed out a sigh of contentment.

'Seeing as how we gotta wait for night-fall before we enter Cannon Falls, why don't we take a rest here for a while? It's too hot to ride,' Adams said.

'Makes sense to me. I ain't felt this cool for a long time.' Clarke grinned.

The two men lay back on the ground and pulled their Stetsons over their faces and within minutes were asleep.

23

Chuck, accompanied by Sally, returned to the sheriff's office with plates of food and two pots of coffee.

'That smells mighty fine,' Reuben said, suddenly feeling really hungry.

'Take a plate through to Anderson,' Reuben said, 'don't want him dying on us.' He grinned.

' 'Bout time, too,' Anderson grumbled.

'You're lucky to get anything,' Chuck said, and slid the plate below the bars of the cell.

'No coffee?' Anderson muttered.

'There's water there, drink that,' Chuck replied and left the cell room.

After they'd finished eating, Reuben spoke up.

'We need to guard Anderson until the sheriff returns. I reckon we take shifts. I don't trust that man any more than I could spit him, sorry ma'am,' Reuben said.

'It's Sally, and I agree with you. The whole town could be in danger if any of the gang find out where he is.' She stopped speaking and looked sheepishly at the floor.

'I don't think there are many — if any — of the gang left.

Except of course, Frank and Jesse James, and I doubt they'd give a damn about Anderson. It would be too risky for them.'

'I agree,' Ely piped up. 'Last report I had was that Frank and Jesse were heading for the Dakotas; they ain't likely to return.'

'Nevertheless, we still need to be vigilant,' Reuben said. 'I'll take first watch, two hours apiece. That OK with you fellas?'

'OK,' said Chuck. 'I'll check out the hotel for you, Ely.'

'No need,' Sally said. 'I have rooms above the Eatery. It's close by and you're welcome to stay. I'll charge the town,' she smiled.

'Thank you kindly, ma'am — sorry

— Sally,' Reuben said, and he was sure he was blushing.

★ ★ ★

Adams and Clarke woke up in the late afternoon. It was stifling hot. The heat from the sun was now rising from the parched ground. Even the small stream felt warm on their feet.

Both men splashed water on their sweaty faces, then dunked their Stetsons in the stream and put them on.

Both horses were quite content, grazing on the grass that grew beside the stream, occasionally taking a drink.

'What time you reckon it is?' Clarke asked.

Adams squinted as he looked up at the sky. The sun's position had moved to the west. 'I'd say around four o'clock,' Adams replied.

'Jeez! That means at least another two hours before the sun sets,' Clarke grumbled.

'Let's get a fire going, and have some

204

coffee. I still got beans and bacon and what's left of the bread. That'll take up an hour or so, then we can get closer to Cannon Falls. And wait.'

'Let's hope some of the gang are there,' Clarke said.

'Well, if they ain't, we'll ride on. Maybe hold up a stage or a train. You never know, we might be better off on our own anyways.' Adams didn't sound convinced as he said those words, but Clarke seemed to take that as a positive sign.

'Grab some kindling and let's get this fire going,' Adams said. 'I'll get the gear together.'

It didn't take long to get the fire started. Adams placed the coffee pot over the flames and waited for the water to boil before adding the Arbuckles. When the coffee was steaming hot, he got the frying pan out, layered it with bacon and it began to sizzle, the aroma making both men hungry.

Adams turned the bacon, then added the beans. They sat back and sipped at the coffee until the food was ready, then both ate from the frying pan.

Finally, they scraped out the fat with bread and drank more coffee.

'That's better,' Adams said. 'Let's break camp and ride on aways.'

'OK, at least we've only got a couple of hours to wait now,' Clarke almost beamed with anticipation.

They saddled up and set off, following the trail of the four horsemen ahead of them, hoping they were heading for Cannon Falls.

They broke into a canter, as the land becoming flatter and greener. Cottonwoods and Joshua trees seemed to thrive here, but there was still the odd cactus and scrub to avoid.

After a few more minutes, they slowed to a trot and Adams called out 'Woah! I see smoke ahead.' Taking out his army 'scope, he soon saw a small shack with smoke bil.lowing from the chimney.

'That Cannon Falls?' Clarke asked.

'Nope, just a shack.'

'You thinkin' what I'm thinkin'?'

Clarke said.

'Oh, yeah. Time we had ourselves a little fun.' Adams gave an evil grin.

24

It took Clarke and Adams only 10 minutes to reach the shack.

'Now let me do the talking,' Adams said. 'You just keep shtum.'

'What the hell does shtum mean?' Clarke asked.

'Jesus H! It means keep your mouth shut. OK?'

'Then why didn't you just say that, 'stead of usin' them there fancy words all the time,' Clarke said sulkily.

'OK, OK. Just let me do the talking, all right?' Adams said, hiding a grin. There was nothing Adams liked more than winding his partner up.

Adams dismounted and knocked on the front door. 'Hello, the house,' he called.

He heard footsteps as the door was opened.

Adams removed his Stetson, and apologized for calling at so late an hour, but then added, 'We're looking for Cannon Falls, ma'am, and wondered if you could give us directions?'

The woman, he guessed, was in her thirties, with auburn-coloured hair tied back in a pony tail. She had a trim body and dark-brown eyes. Dressed in a simple, plain dress, she wore no ring or make-up.

Nevertheless, she was an attractive woman, not a beauty, but Adams thought, dressed and made up, she'd be quite a catch.

'Just follow the trail, mister. Cannon Falls is three miles due west. You can't miss it.' She went to close the door, but Adams stopped her and asked if they might water their animals.

The woman hesitated before replying. She knew the unwritten law of allowing strangers to water their animals. After all, without a horse you were a dead man.

'The trough's over by the barn,' she eventually replied.

Adams replaced his Stetson and tipped it to the woman just as a man entered

209

the hallway brandishing a Winchester.

Without hesitating, Clarke drew his pistol and fired, hitting the man in the chest, sending him flying six feet through the air before he landed with a thump against a table.

The woman screamed and ran to the fallen man.

'What in hell did you do that for?' Adams demanded.

'I thought he was gonna shoot you.'

'You idiot. I was standing in front of the woman. How could he shoot me?'

'I was only tryin' to help,' Clarke said, crestfallen.

'You killed my brother. You killed him.' The woman screamed again.

Adams' face hardened as he approached the woman. He grabbed her and dragged her towards where he thought the bedroom was.

She struggled violently against the taller, stronger man, but his grip held. She realized her left arm was free and felt his holster. She stopped struggling.

'That's better,' Adams said.

As he said that, she grabbed the grip of his Colt, pulled back the hammer and fired off a shot through his holster.

The bullet seared Adams' leg and went through his right foot.

It was his turn to scream. Before he fell to the floor, he caught the woman's face hard with an iron fist which knocked her unconscious.

Clarke immediately dismounted and ran into the house to find his partner lying on the floor, gripping his leg, blood seeping through his jeans and right boot.

'What the hell . . . ?'

'She shot me, what d'you think. With my own damn gun. We need to torch this place and vamoose. Can't leave any witnesses. Find me something I can use as a crutch,' Adams said through gritted teeth.

'You're in luck,' Clarke said. 'There's a walkin' stick hangin' on the door. Shall I fetch it?'

'No, I'll hop over there, shall I? Course you should fetch it.' Idiot, Adams said to himself.

'There you go,' Clarke said, handing the stick to Adams.

'Give me a hand here to stand,' Adams demanded.

Once on his good foot, Adams made for his horse. He mounted up with some difficulty, but found his right foot and leg felt slightly better. Getting his boot off was painful, but he had to see the damage. Luckily, Adams thought, if you could call it luck, the bullet had gone straight through, right between his big toe and the one next to it.

'Smash those oil-lamps and then get the hell outta there,' Adams shouted.

'What about the woman?' Clarke asked.

'What about her? She shot me. She dies.'

Clarke did as he was told, spreading the oil around the front room, leaving a trail to the front door. He struck a Lucifer and tossed it on the oil-soaked wooden veranda.

Rushing to his horse, he mounted up and pulled back to a safer distance.

Both men watched as the flames crept forwards until the whole house was engulfed in flame.

They heard the screams of the woman, and shots as the dead man's Winchester exploded in the heat. Slugs were flying around until the gun was empty.

The screams got louder until the woman emerged from the house. Fire had enveloped her and she took no more than three steps before she fell to the ground.

Dead.

The two men were momentarily horrified at the sight they were witnessing, but Adams wheeled his horse around and yelled, 'Let's get outta here.'

★　★　★

Reuben had spent his time looking through the Wanted posters in the sheriff's desk, as well as those pinned to the wall when the door burst open. A man dressed in a black frock coat, white shirt with a bootlace tie, and black trousers, entered. Reuben thought he looked around sixty, but his ruddy complexion showed he spent a lot of time outside.

'Who the hell are you? And where's the sheriff?' the man barked.

'Fishing with the mayor,' Reuben replied calmly.

'I'm the mayor and I ain't seen hide nor hair of the sheriff today,' the man said.

'Well, where the hell can he be?' Reuben asked as he stared at the mayor.

At that point, a bellow came from the cells at the back of the office. 'I need water!'

'Who you got locked up back there?' the mayor asked.

'Bloody Bill Anderson,' Reuben replied. 'Waiting for the sheriff and the circuit judge.'

The mayor's jaw dropped at the mention of Anderson's name. 'I'm Burt Douglas,' he held his hand out.

Reuben took it and they shook. 'Name's Reuben Chisholm.'

'What's your interest in Anderson?'

214

the mayor asked.

'You mean apart from the fact that he's an ex-Quantrill raider, murderer and rapist?' Reuben didn't have to say anything else.

Ely Watson rushed into the office. 'There's a fire!' he almost shouted.

'In town?' Reuben asked.

'Nope, I reckon two or three miles east of town,' Ely said.

'Sounds like the Turners' place. That's the only home.stead east of here,' the mayor said.

'I'll get Doc Mackay,' Ely said.

'I'll round up some men and we'll ride out there,' the mayor said, and both men rushed out.

'You coming, Reuben?' Ely asked as he came back into the office.

'No. I ain't leaving Anderson. It could be a diversion to break him out — again.'

Ely nodded and ran to the doc's place.

Reuben grabbed hold of a Winchester, making sure it was loaded, and laid it across his lap, behind the desk. Ten minutes later the sound of pounding hoofs passed the office as a small group of men made their way east to the Turner residence.

* * *

Clarke was the first to hear the hoof sounds approaching them. 'Riders comin',' he said quietly to Adams. 'Better get off the trail. Lucky there ain't no moon, they won't see us in the pitch black. I guess they saw the flames.'

Both men turned right and rode about a hundred yards off the trail, making sure their animals didn't panic or make a noise.

The riders quickly passed their position, and Adams and Clarke waited for five minutes, then re-joined the trail to Cannon Falls.

25

The flames had died down to about two or three feet high by the time the riders reached the burned-out house.

The brick chimney collapsed into the scorched remains, sending sparks high into the air and the flames rose higher as it found new things to burn.

Doc Mackay dismounted and walked as close as he could to the body he saw on the steps of the veranda. The heat was too intense to get nearer than ten feet, but he looked at the charred remains of Beth Turner. He almost vomited and backed away.

'That's Beth,' he said. 'I guess Sam is still inside.'

'Well,' the mayor said, 'there's nothing we can do here until the heat dies down a bit, then we'll cover Beth with a tarp, and tomorrow take her body into town.'

'Maybe we'll find, what's his name again?' Ely asked.

'Sam,' the mayor replied. 'Sam Turner.'

'I'll stay here for a while,' Ely said, 'it's still too hot to get a tarp over her, so I'll wait and join you fellas in town later on.'

The men agreed with Ely and rode back to town at a leisurely pace, each man silent with his own thoughts.

★ ★ ★

Clarke and Adams reached the outskirts of Cannon Falls, but had no intention of riding in just yet.

They rode around the town and waited on the northern edge where they had a good view of the layout of the place. The main street, which ran right through the centre of town, was brightly lit by kerosene lanterns, only the smaller streets and alleyways were in darkness.

Adams was peering through his 'scope along Main Street.

'What d'you see, Alex?' asked Clarke.

'What I *don't* see is any people. Seems

218

the whole town is deserted.'

'Well,' Clarke said, peering at his Hunter, 'it is after ten o'clock. I reckon most folk are in bed by now, this being a farmin' area.'

'True,' Adams agreed. 'But it seems strange that no one is about. Even the saloon is closed.'

'Well, that does seem a bit strange,' Clarke agreed.

'Hang on,' Adams said. 'Riders approaching, there's six of them at least. They just dismounted and hitched up outside the sheriff's office.'

'One of the men has just left the office. He's carrying a doc's bag. That's who I gotta see. My foot is damn painful.'

'You see where he's headed?' Clarke asked.

'Sure do. Almost opposite the sheriff's office. There must be a back way. Come on, let's find out.' Adams pulled on the reins to turn his horse to the left. Clarke followed.

★ ★ ★

219

'They're both dead, Reuben,' the mayor said. 'Burned alive by the looks of things. Ely has stayed behind so he can put a tarp over Beth's body, so the night critters don't get what's left of her. It was too hot to get near her.'

'Sounds strangely familiar to me,' Reuben said. 'The two men I'm after are ex-Quantrill men. William Clarke and Alexander Adams. They burned down my neighbour's property — and then mine. My wife was at home, alone. I was too late to save her.'

'I'm sorry to hear that, Reuben. I truly am,' the mayor said, and removed his bowler hat in a sign of respect.

'I think they were following us, thinking we were part of the James-Younger gang. They must have tracked us here,' Reuben said. 'I had a feeling we were being followed.'

'We better get some more men ready,' the mayor said. 'There ain't no way they're gonna ruin this township.'

'We got six Winchesters and two scatter guns here, plus our own weapons. If it is Adams and Clarke,' Reuben said, 'we can expect them at any time, now it's dark.'

Reuben stood and checked the cell. Anderson was sound asleep.

The mayor ran off to wake up some more men, and while he was gone, Ely returned.

'I got her covered up, and used the rocks from the chimney to make sure she'd be safe,' Ely said.

Reuben brought Ely up to date.

'You better warn the doc. His services may well be needed,' Reuben added.

'He at home?' Ely asked.

'Yeah, he left about forty-five minutes ago,' Reuben said.

'I'll go get him,' Ely said, and left the office.

★ ★ ★

Clarke and Adams entered Cannon Falls from the west. The alleyway they chose ran behind the doctor's house.

'Perfect!' Adams said.

221

They hitched their horses to the rear fence and fed them with the oats and barley they had left. 'That should keep them quiet,' Clarke remarked.

As they reached the rear door, they heard a loud banging coming from the front of the house.

The two men stood stock still. Waiting.

The doc, unused as he was to horseback riding, had gone straight to bed and heard absolutely nothing. The banging on the front door stopped, and Adams wondered if whoever it was would try the back door. So again, they waited.

After five minutes, they realized whoever had been banging on the front door, wasn't coming around the back. Clarke forced the back door open. There was a splintering of wood, but it wasn't loud enough to attract any attention.

Once inside the dark house it was easy to find the doctor. His snoring would wake the dead!

Clarke cocked his handgun and rested the barrel on the doctor's head.

'Time to wake up, old man. You got

some doctoring to do here,' Clarke grated.

Doc Mackay's eyes snapped open and he stared at the bearded figure leaning over him, gun in hand.

'You pull that trigger and you'll get no doctorin',' he said calmly.

Clarke released the hammer and put the gun back in its holster.

'OK? My pal here done shot hisself in the foot; damn fool forgot to put the safety on,' Clarke said, surprising Adams that he had the sense to make up a good story.

'Pass me my dressin' gown,' the doc said, as he sat up.

⋆ ⋆ ⋆

'Strange,' Ely said as he entered the sheriff's office. 'Can't get any reply from the doc.'

'He's probably sound asleep,' Reuben said as he walked to the front door. 'He's more used to his buggy than . . . ' Reuben stopped in mid-sentence.

'His light in the surgery has just been

lit,' Reuben said. 'I could've sworn I saw two bearded men standing behind him as he closed the drapes.'

'You think it's Adams and Clarke?' Ely asked.

'I don't think it is, I *know* it's them! They must have sneaked round the back. Go find the mayor and get those men together. I'll see if there are horses behind the doc's place. If there are, I'll lead them away so there's no escape. Make sure two or three men get on the rooftops opposite and the rest take cover. I want no shooting until I say so. OK?'

Ely left the office once more, and Reuben filled his Colt. Like most cowboys, he only loaded five bullets in his gun, leaving an empty chamber under the hammer. Satisfied, he grabbed a Winchester, cocked it, already having filled it with .45s, the same as his handgun.

He moved towards the door and took a surreptitious look at the doctor's house, making sure the drapes were still closed; then stealthily crossed Main Street and headed down an unlit alleyway, took a right-hand turn and saw two horses tied to the back fence. He unhooked both animals and mounted one, leading the other horse behind him.

He walked the beasts to the end of the alleyway and across Main Street to the rear of the sheriff's office, where he dismounted and tied the animals to a hitch rail.

Reuben returned to the office and waited for Ely and however many men he and the mayor could round up. It was ten minute's later when eight men crowded into the sheriff's office and Reuben outlined his plan.

They had to be careful and patient as the doc was involved, so there was to be no random shooting at the house. Reuben scanned the faces of the men and noted their weapons. He picked three men with Winchesters and told them to get on the roof of the jailhouse. One of them to stay there, and the other two to fan out onto other buildings left and right, with a good view of the doctor's house.

'I can't stress enough how important it is that no one starts shooting until I give the order. These two men are ruthless killers and rapists, and they'll think nothing of using the doc as a shield, or killing as many of you as they can.' Reuben paused: 'I've corralled their horses, so they can't escape. I'll stand at the corner of the alleyway behind the doc's house, and when I see them coming out, I'll start shooting. That's your signal to wait to see if they turn tail and use the front of the house. Is that clear?'

All the men nodded, one or two had apprehension etched on their faces, but Reuben thought that natural for townsfolk who'd never been involved in such a situation.

'The rest of you take cover on the boardwalk and keep your heads down, and whatever happens, don't panic. OK, let's move out.'

Reuben then made his way back to the rear of the doctor's house and waited in the shadows.

26

'I'm gonna have to cut that boot off,' the doctor said.

'Hell no!' Adams said. 'Pull it off.'

'That'll hurt like hell,' the doc replied, 'but OK, if that's what you want.'

Doc Mackay reached into his big black bag and took out a bottle of laudanum. 'Take a coupla swigs of this, it'll ease the pain.'

Adams gulped the liquid as if it were water.

'Woah! Hold up there,' the doc said. 'That stuff is dan.gerous.' He took the bottle back, and took out his whiskey bottle. Taking a swig himself, he then allowed Adams two quick gulps, before pouring some in the hole in Adams' right boot.

Adams gritted his teeth, but couldn't stop a loud groan as the whiskey burned his wound.

'You,' the doc pointed at Clarke, 'hold

his shoulders down,' and he handed Adams a length of leather. 'Put this between your teeth. This is gonna sting a tad!'

The medico grabbed the heel and toe of the boot and pulled. He pulled hard, and slowly the boot slid off the groaning man's foot. Next came the sock. This was just as painful, as the dried blood had stuck the sock to his toes. The doctor poured some water over the sock to soften the blood. Then, in one swift move, pulled the sock free, and Clarke found it difficult to keep Adams still.

'Well, that's the worst part over. You're lucky, young man,' the doc said. 'The bullet passed between your toes. No bones broken, or missin' toes. Just flesh wounds. Soon have those bound and your foot bandaged up. You won't be wearin' a boot for a few weeks but if you've a spare sock, you can wear it.'

'I don't have any spare socks, Doc,' Adams said.

'Why am I not surprised,' the doc replied. 'I'll give you one o' mine. On second thoughts, I'll give you a pair.'

The doc left the room and went to his bedroom and rummaged around for an old pair of socks.

'Shall I kill him now?' Clarke said.

'Hell, no! He's done my foot. We'll pay him and leave, scout the town awhile and see what we can find out about the James-Younger gang, or what's left of it.'

'OK,' Clarke replied, 'if you think that's best.'

'We don't want to make our presence felt. You kill the doc and the town will be on guard. We gotta keep quiet,' Adams said as the doctor returned.

'Thanks, Doc,' Adams said, smiling. 'How much do I owe you?'

'Five dollars would cover it, if that's all right with you?'

'Fine by me. Thanks, Doc,' Adams handed over the money as Mackay slid the sock on and passed the right boot to Clarke.

'There you go. I got a spare stick you can use, try and keep your weight off the foot for a week or two, OK?'

'Thanks again, Doc, we'll be on our way,' Adams said as he swung his legs off the table and, holding the stick in his

left hand, hobbled towards the back door.

'It's easier goin' out the front door,' Mackay said.

'It's OK, Doc, our horses are out back.'

'Take care, fellas,' the doc said, and watched them leave.

It didn't take them long to discover their missing animals.

* * *

Reuben was ready as he watched a shard of light dimly light up the path from the doctor's house.

Two men stood there wondering what the hell had happened to their animals. 'You sure you tied 'em up real good?' Adams asked Clarke.

'Sure, I did. I ain't stupid.' Clarke was affronted. 'Let's get back inside. Some-one must have seen us,' Adams said.

'Or the light from the doc's surgery,'

Clarke said.

'Whatever,' Adams said, 'let's get back inside.'

The doc had just taken his dressing gown off as the two men burst into his bedroom.

'What the — ' the doc stood, shocked.

'Who'd you tell?' Adams asked.

'Tell what?' Mackay was perplexed. 'How could I tell anyone anythin'. You woke me up, remember?'

Adams looked at Clarke. 'He's right, there's no way he could have told anyone,' Adams said.

'So, we got ourselves a hostage.' Clarke grinned. 'No one's gonna start shootin' while the doc's here, are they.'

★ ★ ★

Damn!' Reuben said to himself.

He ran back to Main Street and waited there for a moment, before crossing back to the sheriff's office. The men on the boardwalk wondered what the hell was going on and, one by one, they entered the office.

'They went back inside the doc's place,' Reuben said. 'But I got a good look at them and it's definitely Adams and Clarke.' He took out two Wanted posters and spread them on the desk.

'Anyone see these two tonight?' Reuben asked.

They all shook their heads. Most of them were either getting ready for bed or already asleep when Ely and the mayor had called for their help.

'So, they snuck into town. Why? Who are they after?' Reuben then sat in silence.

'They could have been tracking us,' Ely said. 'Though God knows why.'

'They thought we were members of the gang,' Reuben said.

'What gang?' one of the men asked.

'The James-Younger gang, or what's left of them.'

'Why would they want to get them?' another man asked.

'These two are ex-Quantrill raiders, they didn't want to get them, they wanted to join them.'

'So, what do we do now?' Ely asked.

'We wait for them to make their move. They can't stay in there forever,' Reuben said.

'Keep the men on the rooftops, but I want two men at each end of the alleyway behind the doc's house. Ely and I will stay here and keep an eye on the front. If they're gonna try and make a break for it using the doc as a hostage, they'll come out the front door with him as a shield.'

Reuben looked at each of the men eye-to-eye, then said: 'OK, let's do this.'

The men dispersed quickly, taking up their positions.

Everything that could be ready, was ready. Now all they had to do was wait.

* * *

'OK, Doc, get dressed, we're quitting this here town and you're gonna help us get out.' Adams glared at Mackay with such intensity that the doc feared for his life if he didn't do what he was told.

He dressed.

'Clarke, check outside, see what's out there,' Adams ordered.

Clark went through to the doc's living room and peered out the window. As far as he could see, there was no move. ment, no sign of life at all. In fact, it was pitch black.

'Nothin' movin' out there at all,' Clarke said, picking up his Winchester and checking the magazine. It was full.

'Where's the livery?' Adams asked Doc Mackay.

'Behind the sheriff's office, down the far alleyway,' Mackay replied.

'OK. That's where we're headed. You lead the way. My gun will be on your back. One false move, one sound and you're a dead man. Got it?' Adams said, the menace in his voice sent cold shivers up the doctor's back.

Slowly, Clarke cracked the front door, half expecting a hail of bullets. But nothing happened. He opened the door fully and took a step forward, then Adams pushed the doc in front of him, his Colt pressing against Mackay's spine.

All three stood on the front porch for a matter of seconds before stepping down onto Main Street, heading to their right.

'Here they come,' Reuben whispered.

He and Ely had their rifles trained on Clarke as he was an easy target standing to the doctor's right. Adams, stick in his left hand and his right hidden behind the doc, was to his left.

'We gotta take Adams out first,' Ely said, moving his rifle slightly to the right. 'I reckon he's got a gun in his right hand.'

'Reckon you're right,' Reuben agreed, 'let's hope no one starts shooting, otherwise the doc's a gonna.'

'I can see all of Clarke,' Reuben said, 'but only half of Adams.'

From the other side of the office, Ely said, 'I got three-quarters of Adams. If'n the doc don't change direction, we should fire on three.'

'Try not to kill them,' Reuben said. 'I want them alive to face trial.'

'I'll do my best,' Ely replied.

'OK. One — two — three.'

Ely got Adams in the hip at the top of his left leg. He collapsed immediately, losing hold of the walking stick.

Clarke managed to fire a shot that shattered the office window, but Reuben's aim was as true as Ely's. The doc just stood still, looking like the statue of a frightened rabbit.

The four men based at the rear alleyway to the doc's house, rushed onto Main Street, ready to shoot. But Reuben was on the boardwalk and shouted for everyone to hold their fire.

'You OK, Doc?' Reuben called out.

'I-I think so. I'm not hit if that's what you mean, but I peed in my pants.'

There was a wail of laughter as Mackay made his way back to his house.

'You better bring them back in,' the doc said over his shoulder. 'In about five minutes!'

Reuben and Ely disarmed both men writhing on the ground. Adams had been shot more in the buttocks than his hip, and Clarke was hit high on the right thigh.

'Who the hell are you?' Adams gasped.

'I'm Ely Watson, Pinkerton agent. This here is Reuben Chisholm.'

'You killed the Carver family and burned their house down, then you killed my wife and burned our house down, too,' Reuben said through gritted teeth. 'And now you're both gonna hang.'

'We never killed your wife,' Clarke said. 'There was no one at the second house. We just took some vittles and ammo and rode on.'

'You telling me the truth?' Reuben asked.

'Mister, whoever you are, I'm lyin' here with a slug in my leg at the mercy of anyone who decides to finish me off. Why would I lie?'

'Reuben, we better get these two into my surgery, so's I can get these slugs out,' Doc Mackay said. 'There's a stretcher behind the door. I'd better see to Clarke first. Adams just has a slug in his backside.'

The stretcher was brought out and Clarke was carried into the surgery and laid on the operating table.

Reuben followed on, and while the doc cut Clarke's jeans off, Reuben went through his pockets to try and find any identification.

He brought out a sheriff's badge.

'Well, at least we now know what happened to the sheriff,' Reuben said. 'You kill him?'

'Ain't no point in denyin' it,' Clarke said, pain etched on his face as the doc got to work.

'Now I need to find Grace,' Reuben said. 'All these years I been chasing you two and I should have been looking for her.'

'You weren't to know,' Ely said. 'If she is still alive, we'll find her.'

'Thanks, Ely. I appreciate the help.'

Four men entered the surgery, carrying Adams and laid the stretcher on the floor in a corner out of the way.

The doctor worked on; he used no form of anaesthetic as he dug the bullet out. He wasn't going to waste his whiskey on the killer of his friend, the sheriff.

Removing the bullet, he poured some black powder in the wound, struck a Lucifer, and Clarke nearly hit the ceiling. Then, having sewn the wound, he bandaged it and told the men to lay him on the floor and move Adams onto the table.

He went through the same procedure, taking no notice of Adams' moans, and finished his work.

'That's it. Take 'em to the cells,' the doc said, taking a cloth to clean his bloodied hands before taking a swig of whiskey.

'There's nothing more to do tonight,' Reuben said, and thanking the men for their help, suggested they all get some sleep.

There was no way Reuben would get any sleep that night. His wife, Grace, might still be alive. A thought that had never occurred to him, so convinced was he that she had been killed, just like the Carver family.

Now he had hope. Now he had something to live for.

27

The night sky began to recede as the sun slowly rose in the east, sending shards of red-white beams across the land.scape.

There was a knock at the door and Sally stood on the boardwalk with fresh coffee and three plates of ham and eggs.

'Thought you'd need some food,' she said.

Ely, smelling the coffee and food, opened his eyes and yawned, before standing up and stretching. 'That's mighty fine of you, ma'am,' he said.

'I'll bring the prisoners some food a little later,' she demurred.

Reuben thanked her and put the tray on the desk.

Sally left the office, and Ely was certain she was blush.ing, although whether it was because of him or Reuben, he didn't know.

The two men tucked in just as the mayor arrived and grabbed the third plate. 'That Sally sure cooks a good breakfast,' he said as he sat.

'So,' Ely began. 'What's the plan?'

'I need to find Grace — if she's still alive. It's been over five years.'

'Where the hell do we start?' Ely asked.

'I'm heading south,' Reuben said. 'Back to my old homestead. That's where it started, and that's where I'll begin.'

Mopping up the egg yolk and ham fat, Reuben finished eating, drained his coffee mug and stood.

'You leaving right now?' the mayor asked.

Before Reuben could answer, the door burst open and a townsman Reuben didn't know rushed in.

'Mr Chisholm, sir. You better come outside. NOW!'

Without hesitation, Reuben rushed through the door, gun in hand.

'You won't need the gun,' a soft, female voice said.

★ ★ ★

241

Reuben stood stock-still, hardly believing his eyes.

'Grace! Grace, is that you?'

She dismounted and rushed towards her husband. They hugged and then a long, luxurious kiss followed.

'But . . . how . . . I mean . . .' Reuben was speechless.

He led her by the hand into the sheriff's office, poured two cups of coffee, and the mayor and Ely made a subtle exit, leaving them alone.

'I saw the riders approaching and instinctively knew they were up to no good by the way they were galloping. I guess I panicked at first, but then I saddled up and rode south as fast as I could. I found shelter and waited two days. No one had followed me, so I slowly made my way back to the homestead. It was burned down and there was no sign of you. But the buggy was there, provisions rotting in the sun.

'I was sure you were dead, but then I noticed the wagon's horse was missing, and your saddle from the corral fence, so I knew you were alive. I didn't know what to do. I rode into town, but no one seemed to know where you'd gone, so I stayed with Maud Whitely. You remember her? She owned the milliner's store.

'Days turned into weeks and weeks into months and finally months into years. I had to do something as it was obvious you weren't coming back.'

'But how did you end up here?' Reuben asked.

'I often went back to our home, but never saw any sign of you until the sheriff rode with me one day and pointed at the ground. It was high summer, and the ground was rock hard, but there were old tracks there. I saw the tracks of two horses, obviously old, and then I found a third. I knew it was you. I don't know how, but I did. They headed north, so did I.'

'But Cannon Falls?'

'I rode for three days and ended up in a small town, I can't remember its name, but there was a newspaper there, and a story about a failed bank robbery in

243

Northfield. Your name was mentioned.'

'So you went to Northfield?'

'Yes. But you'd already left, chasing someone called Anderson. You were talked of as a bit of a hero for captur.ing this man, but then he was busted out of jail, which was why you had left North-field, determined to get him back.

'I hung around for three days, but you never returned, Eventually, I discovered which way you had headed, so I went north. I'd become quite a good tracker, believe me, I could read sign. There were a lot of tracks, some older than others, so I knew you or someone was following the older tracks.

'I lost them for long periods, but I carried on up the trail and came across two campsites, miles apart. South of the first campsite, I came across a buggy with a grazing pony. I couldn't see any-one nearby, so I rode on. I didn't know where you were headed for, but I kept to the trail, and here I am, five years later.'

Reuben stood and hugged his wife again, tears running down both their faces. It was the mayor who interrupted their reunion.

He coughed in the doorway.

'I thought you might want this,' the mayor said, holding the sheriff's badge towards Reuben. 'What do you say, Sheriff?'

Grace took the badge and pinned it on Reuben's vest. 'He says yes,' she replied for him.

Reuben smiled.

Cannon Falls had a new sheriff and, once the circuit judge had visited and condemned both Clarke and Adams, Reuben and Grace settled down to a peaceful and happy life.